MENDING CHRISTMAS
with the billionaire

OTHER BOOKS BY LORIN GRACE

American Homespun Series
Waking Lucy
Remembering Anna
Reforming Elizabeth
Healing Sarah

Artists & Billionaires
Mending Fences
Mending Walls
Mending Images
Mending Words
Mending Hearts

Artists & Billionaires 2

MENDING CHRISTMAS
with the billionaire

LORIN GRACE

CURRANT
CREEK PRESS

Cover Design © 2018 LJP Creative
Photos © iStock, Deposit Photos

Formatting by LJP Creative
Edits by Eschler Editing

Published by Currant Creek Press
North Logan, Utah

Second edition: August 2018
ISBN: 978-0-9984110-7-1

For Cindy
Não há nada nesta terra a ser mais
valorizada do que a verdadeira amizade.

ARACELI DROPPED HER BACKPACK ON the kitchen table. "I hate finals!"

Tessa patted her back. "It could be worse. You could have to grade them. Why I ever took on teaching The Elements of Glass and History of Stained Glass in America, I'll never know."

"Remember, you are the idiot who asked your students to write a paper due at the end of the term." Candace opened the Rembrandt-painted cupboard and retrieved a glass. "Now you know why most teachers request them before Thanksgiving break."

Araceli opened the fridge. "At least I didn't have any of those this term. But I feel as if the entire contents of the Louvre are stuck inside my head trying to get out and I can't remember which one was painted in 1592."

Tessa didn't look up from her computer. "Carracci's Virgin, or Caravaggio's Boy Peeling Fruit, but Boy is in Rome, not Paris."

Candace sat at the table, her short red hair and green T-shirt giving her an elfish air. "I still don't know how you remember so much. It's been four years since you took Renaissance Art History."

"Spending most of the year in Europe helped me place them. So, what have you decided to do for Christmas break?" Tessa snatched one of Araceli's cookies.

Araceli pulled her plate away. "I'm going to lock myself in my bedroom and read novels. Then I am going to sketch a Boston blizzard by leaving the paper untouched."

"My dad confirmed this morning that he is coming here for Christmas as my sister and her husband are off to Hawaii. With the empty room, I figured it worked. Did you two get Mandy's invitation? New Year's Gala hosted by C & O in Chicago?" Candace scrolled through her phone. "I don't want to go alone, and I am not bringing a plus-one."

Tessa checked her calendar. "I'll be back by then. Mom is going to Connecticut to celebrate Christmas with Grandma, and I can only stand her couch for so long. I don't go to Park City with Dad until the second or third." Tessa's computer chimed. She turned her attention to the email. She checked the From line twice. "It's from Gavin."

"Delete it!" her roommates said in unison.

"The subject is 'Help! Broken Window in NY.'" Tessa opened the email. "He says a church in Blue Pines had one of its windows damaged by a drone. They need it fixed by Christmas. The window is over 120 years old. He can't do the repair job because of his wedding."

"Of course not, the slime."

"Hey, guys, remember, I did kiss him back. I just didn't know he'd kissed all the other interns, too." Tessa held up a hand. "And he does get points for tossing a sweet job my way. Look at these photos." Tessa turned her laptop around. "I needed another repair job for my MFA to be complete, and this works perfectly. I can do it, go see Mom and Grandma for a couple of days, be back for the Gala, and still go to Park City with my dad for a few days before school starts again."

Candace shook her head. "Sometimes, Tess, I think you try to keep yourself too busy."

Sean Cavanagh dusted the old organ's keyboard. It wouldn't help. It wouldn't make $4,000 appear. There just wasn't enough in the church's building fund to pay for the repairs the old lady needed. Especially not now with the Nativity window broken. Two weeks ago he'd boxed up the trumpet pipes to send out to be fixed in time for Christmas Eve. That same afternoon the teens had sent their drones careening into the building.

"Sean, there you are. I have good news. I won't have to dip into my rainy-day fund after all." Sean's grandfather leaned on his cane as he came up the aisle, his black shirt and starched clerical collar ironed to perfection. "I got an answer from Gavin. His college friend agreed to do the windows and not charge for his time. Someone by the name of Doyle will be here Monday afternoon or Tuesday morning. We can have our window for Christmas. I need to go speak with Margo about a room. If someone is willing to do the job without pay, we can at least give them room and board. She never lets out the old housekeeper's room—too small and cramped."

"Granda, are you sure Gavin said this Doyle would work pro bono? After all, he bid $8,500 to do the work himself."

"Yes, he said Doyle was working on an MFA and needed another project. And we would only be expected to pay for the glass and whatever else they use to repair the window. He still says we should invest in a new protective window or glazing."

Sean came down from the organ loft. "But if the glass needs to come from some special place like Gavin suggested, it could be more than $1,000. All we have is an estimate from a guy you met once and now his word that some other guy is going to donate $7k worth of work."

"Your problem is you have too little faith."

"And yours is you have too much. Don't you see, Granda, the pews sit empty most Sundays? The big denominations have other means to fall back on if their donations fail, but what does your little church have?"

"We have Christmas."

"But it's not enough anymore." Sean ran his hand down his face. The argument was far from new. More than a century ago these walls served a noble purpose providing both Catholics and Protestants a place to worship. For a few brief years, this little building may have been the only place on earth the sects got along. But as the number of congregations grew and the community recovered from the fire that had destroyed the north half of town, they'd moved into their own buildings, leaving the little Church of the Nativity to fill the tiny gap of nondenominational and community Christmas services and to remind the members of all the churches what they had in common.

Sean's grandfather sat down on the front pew. "Christmas will always be enough. It always has been."

"That is why you can't afford an organist?" *Not that there is much of an organ to play.* Explaining why he could not do the needed repairs was as futile as all the other arguments. Angels were not going to come down and sing with the organ for Christmas services.

"Why should I pay for one when I have you? Aren't you the best in New York? And the way you can repair an organ, I know it will play with no dead notes." Granda patted Sean's hand and then shuffled out of the building.

"But how much longer do I have you?" Sean whispered the question to the empty sanctuary.

two

AFTER HER GPS TRIED TO send her into the center of the Hudson River, Tessa followed the green signs to Blue Pines. She was tempted to toss the app in the water where the soothing British accent insisted she go. The trip from northern Indiana should have taken her just over ten hours. It had taken closer to fifteen. Driving in clear weather with no traffic jams, not even in Pennsylvania, the only explanation for the delay was that the GPS app had spent most of its time getting her lost.

"Never follow directions from a guy, Gertie." She patted the seat of her car.

At last, a "Welcome to Blue Pines" sign appeared. The steeples of three churches lit the sky. Tomorrow would be soon enough to figure out which one contained the broken window. She pulled into a gas station, filled up, then got directions to the inn. Apparently the town boasted only one inn, which the attendant assured her she couldn't miss. He didn't know her or Gertie very well.

Fortunately he was correct. Located on the river, the inn was easy to find and had an empty parking space.

Tessa guessed the building hailed from the 1830s. If the walls could talk, what tales would they tell?

A short woman with gray hair manned the desk—the old-fashioned kind with little mailboxes on the wall behind her. Keys hung from one of the boxes on a large brass ring.

Tessa set down her suitcase and returned the smile the woman offered. "Tessa Doyle. I believe a Reverend Cavanagh made the reservation."

"I'm Margo." The woman bent her head and studied the paper register. "Where is your husband?"

"My husband?"

"Yes, your husband. The reverend made the reservation for a *Mr.* Doyle. Perhaps you are his daughter?"

"I am not married, and my father is not with me." Tessa scrolled through her phone until she found the email. "Here is the email I received."

Margo perched a set of reading glasses on the end of her nose. "Well, isn't this a surprise. You are the one who is going to fix our window?"

"Our window?" Tessa looked around the lobby.

"The one at our church."

"Oh, yes, I am."

Margo appraised her. "Well, you are a breath of fresh air. Those Cavanaghs won't know what hit them, but I am sure, sweetie, that you are an answer to at least one prayer." Margo stood and grabbed the key from the last box. "I apologize—this is our tiniest room, but there is a bathroom. We don't have call to use this much, but when the reverend asked us to donate a room to help with your costs, it was the least we could do."

Tessa took the key with its massive ring.

"Second floor, middle of the hall. Did you get something to eat? The dining room is closed, but the cook may still have some of her corn chowder on the stove." Margo had crossed the lobby before she finished the sentence.

"Maybe some bread?" Tessa followed. Chowder wasn't her favorite.

The dining room had been cleared for the night. Margo called to an unseen person beyond a door Tessa assumed led to the kitchen. "Anything left we can share with a guest?"

An answer came almost immediately. "Some tomato bisque and garlic bread sticks. Oh, and some of our famous cheesecake."

Margo turned back to Tessa with a smile. "Since the dining room is closed, you'll need to eat it in your room. Go on up, dear, and I'll get it delivered as soon as it's warmed."

"How much do I owe you?"

"This one is on the house. All leftovers, anyway."

The room was tiny but not uncomfortably so. The wrought-iron bed could only be called three-quarter size. Too wide for a twin and too narrow for a double. A soft-looking chair sat next to a window and desk. More personal space than in the dorm her freshman year, it would serve nicely for the next couple weeks. A slip of paper on the desk indicated the Wi-Fi password was "guest." The closet was only large enough to hold five hangers worth of clothes. Good thing she did most of her work in jeans and T-shirts.

When the anticipated knock came at the door, she opened it to find a teenage boy holding a tray. "Margo says you can't tip me because it was my drone."

"Your drone?"

"Yeah, lady, the one that flew through the window you are here to repair. Are you going to take your food or what?"

Tessa reached for the tray, and the surly boy disappeared down the hall before she could thank him.

"I told you, Granda, no repair person. I'd wait longer with you, but I need to catch the noon train into the city." Sean put the broom back in the closet.

"When will you ever learn patience? The noon train won't be here for over three hours. Margo told me Doyle got in late last night. I am sure he will be here soon. Now, if you don't mind, I need to visit the throne room." Reverend Cavanagh vanished into the small corridor leading to the bathrooms.

Sean grabbed the dustcloth to wipe off the backs of the pews. He noticed the O'Connell kids had eaten bread and jam during Sunday morning's service.

"Excuse me."

Sean turned to see a blonde wisp of a woman standing two feet inside the door. "Can I help you?"

"I am looking for a Mr. Cavanagh."

"I'm Sean Cavanagh."

A tiny frown settled between her eyebrows. "May I see the broken window?"

Sean waved his arm to the far side of the sanctuary. "Sure, look all you want. Just don't touch."

"But I am going to need to touch it."

"Whatever for?"

"If I'm going to fix it, I'll need to touch it."

"*You* fix the window?"

The woman's chin lifted. "Of course. Why else would I be here?"

"What happened to Doyle?"

"Mr. Cavanagh, I happen to be Miss Tessa Doyle."

"But you are a woman."

"I have been all my life. Is this a problem for you?" She moved her hands to her hips, her eyes flashing. They were almost the same color blue as the glass in Mary's robe. "Are you objecting to me repairing your window because I am female?" The woman half turned as if to leave.

Dropping the dustcloth, Sean worked his way out of the pews. "No—yes. I mean, I thought you were a man."

"We exchanged emails for nearly a week, and not once did you read my email address and think I might be female?"

"Your email address?"

"Glassgirl@college.com"

"I never saw your emails." *Can hair that color be real*? It didn't look dyed. Sean stepped closer.

"You didn't get them? Then who answered them? Who made the reservations at the inn?"

Sean searched his mind for the name she'd tossed at him and gave up. He reached her side before she could leave. "Miss Doyle, I am sorry. I'm surprised you are not a man. My Granda kept talking about Doyle, so I expected a man."

"Granda?"

"Grandpa, Grandfather, Grandad, I've always called him Granda. Part of my Irish, I guess. Everyone else calls him Reverend."

She tilted her head and looked up at him. "Aren't you the reverend?"

Sean shook his head. Preaching was the one profession he'd denounced, even as a toddler. "Nope."

"So you never read my emails?" Her arms dropped to her side.

"Not a one." Sean couldn't suppress a grin as the fire in her eyes cooled. "Perhaps we could start again, Miss Doyle. Would you like to inspect the broken window?"

"Is your grandfather here?"

Sean nodded to the still-empty corridor. "He will join us in a minute. The window is over here."

three

DUCT TAPE. IT COULDN'T BE. But it was. Tessa hoped the tape was one of the cheap kinds that didn't stick well. The residue would be a pain to remove. "Was there a protective glazing outside?"

"Glazing?"

How often did she need to remind herself to use words people knew? "Glass—a clear window—was there one?"

"*Was* being the operative word." He gave her a crooked smile, much like her favorite actor's.

Candace! I need one of your lectures now! Brown eyes, dark-auburn hair, and the slightest shadow of a beard—a dangerous combination even if he seemed to have an issue with her. The navy sweater fit fantastic on him too. But she was only going to be here two weeks, tops. No reason to know him any better. If only her mind could relay the message to the rest of her body. *Focus, girl, focus!*

"A drone hit it? I wouldn't think that could cause so much damage." Tessa tried to trace a large crack only to realize it was a shadow from the broken glass on the other side.

"The boys were racing their drones. They claim they raced them at speeds over one hundred miles per hour." Sean shifted behind her, the movement enough to make her aware of his body's warmth.

What part of her had missed the memo? She was avoiding men for the rest of the year.

A tapping sound came from across the room. Sean left her side.

"Granda, let me introduce *Miss* Doyle."

"Miss Doyle? I thought Gavin said you were a man." The older man was dressed like she expected a reverend to be dressed, plus he held a thick sweater in his hand.

"You know Gavin Beaufontaine?"

The reverend shook his head. "I only met him once, but since he is Mrs. Carmichael's grand-nephew's friend, he came out as a favor to look at the damage. Can't wrap my mouth around that last name of his, so he's just Gavin."

Tessa issued a sigh of relief. She didn't want to get any closer to Gavin than his last email.

"He gave me an estimate, but it nearly made poor Sean's eyes pop out of his head. Then he told me he knew the man for the job. I'm sorry, miss. That is what he said. Never dawned on me he would refer to someone as cute as you are as a man." The reverend shook his head. Tessa chose to give the older man the benefit of the doubt. He continued. "Told me his friend Doyle would do the job for the cost of materials."

It was the second time in the last few minutes she'd heard she would be donating her time and labor. But, looking at the old man, she couldn't bring herself to correct him. He'd arranged for her hotel at no charge and it did check the box for her MFA, so she could live with it.

"Did he give you an estimate for the materials?" Tessa needed to know how badly Gavin had messed with her life this time."

Sean spoke up. "He said a couple thousand."

Tessa nodded but made no comment. At least he'd estimated high, unless the bid included the new protective glazing.

The grandfather chimed in. "He talked about needing to go to a Tiffany's supplier to look through their old glass records and order special glass."

"Why can't you buy some off the internet? Those prices are not nearly as high as what he quoted us." Sean crossed his arms.

Tessa bit her lip. "I could get the glass off a web discount store, but it wouldn't be the same. See this piece in Mary's robe? It is called drapery glass. In order to match it, I need to find glass of similar color and texture. If I use a flat piece purchased from "Glass-R-Us," it will never look right. But you should know a special order of this glass won't be cheap, as we would need to buy an entire case of glass." *And I doubt they could get it here before Christmas.*

Tap, tap. The reverend's cane demanded attention. "Can't you glue it? Down at the hardware store they carry special glass glue like they use on chipped windshields."

"Yes, Reverend, there is a special type of epoxy, and I may end up using it on this painted hand, and maybe here." Joseph, Mary, and the baby Jesus' face had all been spared breakage, but the duct tape on the painted glass might cause even more damage. She hoped she could remove the tape from the hand without destroying the piece. "But it isn't like gluing a teacup handle back together. Well, I guess it is—the glued piece will never be exactly right. Epoxy is used when it would be more noticeable to replace the glass and there is enough glass to glue."

Sean moved to her side. "Where are you going to do the repairs?"

Tessa traced the edge of the frame with her finger. "I am not sure yet. This border is built in separate square frames. This third frame received most of the damage. It makes sense to remove this frame and work on it flat, as the lead came has been contorted so much."

"Lead came?" the reverend asked.

"Yes, sorry," she said, reminding herself again to speak in layman's terms and pointing to a section of the window. "It's this slender, grooved rod that holds the panes together. I need to look on the outside first to make sure I am correct, but I believe I can remove this pane without causing more damage. And I need to make something to keep the other panes from shifting while I work."

"Like in those remodeling shows where they build a temporary wall?"

Tessa glanced back at the reverend. "Something like that. Have you already ordered a new protective glazing for the outside?"

Reverend Cavanagh shook his head.

"It looks like this old glazing was added in the seventies. Did it get broken then, too?"

Sean laughed. "My father hit a home run right through the little lamb."

Tessa inspected the animal. "This is a superior repair job. May I go see the outside? Do you have a ladder?"

"I'll show you." Sean offered.

The reverend shifted in his seat. "Don't miss your train."

Sean led Tessa around the back of the church. She stood on her tiptoes as if the extra few inches would make a difference as she studied the base of the window.

"I'll go get a ladder." Sean left her there. Why did he follow her around anyway? Even if she had agreed to do the job pro bono, she'd seemed surprised when Granda mentioned the lack of pay. But she hadn't argued. What was her plan?

When he returned, Tessa climbed up and ran her fingers over the stone windowsill.

"Careful, there still may be glass shards up there."

She pulled her hand back. "I hadn't thought of that."

Sean set up the ladder.

Tessa steadied herself at the top and pulled a small sketchbook out of her bag, then handed it down to him. "Would you mind taking down a few measurements?"

Sean expected her to measure the entire window, but she only measured sections. Some of them more than once. She pulled out a magnifying glass and inspected further, then she took out her phone and snapped a few photos.

Tessa hopped down and held out her hand for the sketchbook. "You have very neat handwriting. Thank you." She slid the book back into her bag.

"Why are you doing this?" Sean had to ask.

"Well, I need measurements—"

"No, why did you agree to do this job for nothing? I saw the shock on your face when Granda mentioned it. Were you not planning on working for free?"

Tessa tucked a strand of hair behind her ear. "Not exactly, but after Margo didn't charge me for dinner, breakfast, or the hotel room, it kind of made sense to do my portion as a gift too. Besides I suspect it is very difficult to say no to your grandfather."

"But people don't do that." Sean folded the ladder and lifted it to his shoulder.

Tessa moved back. "Then you must not know Margo very well. I assure you she did."

"Of course Margo did. I mean people who aren't from here just don't donate their time to help others."

Tessa squinted as she looked up at him. "You must have minimal experience with the rest of the world. Statistically, Americans are among the most giving people in the world in both time and money. I've lived in six states—toured all of them as well as Canada and most of Europe. I don't know what your problem is, but people do help others. I suspect from the condition of the church, it isn't exactly a flourishing enterprise. If I choose to donate my time, I don't see where you can get off questioning my motives."

She stared him in the eye for a long moment before turning and making her way to the back door of the church.

The chimes over at the Presbyterian church began to play. Great. He was about to miss his train.

TESSA LOCATED THE REVEREND IN a dusty cubbyhole of an office. Books and papers filled every conceivable shelf and corner. At first she thought the room was empty, until Reverend Cavanagh's voice floated over the piles on his desk

"Did you find a ladder?"

"Yes, Sean got one for me."

"And?"

"You should ban drones from the church grounds." Tessa tried to keep a smile in her voice. "Also, whoever advised you to put the protective glazing on all those years ago probably saved the window from complete ruin."

"Nice to hear. The board balked at spending the extra money, but in the end, the Goodings donated the funds—something about Ansley being the one to pitch the ball." Reverend Cavanagh pushed a pile of books to the side, giving Tessa a view of his face.

"So, you were already working—I mean ministering, er, whatever—here the last time the window was broken?"

The older man chuckled. "Yes, I took over for my father full-time a year or two before my son, Cameron, hit that ball. Thought about getting the window insured then, but the Lord provided, so we didn't. The insurance company wanted a special rider for each window, and that was too expensive. Ten windows and double for the rose window."

"So you are telling me there is no insurance on the windows?" The reverend shook his head.

No wonder he'd hoped she would do the work pro bono.

"Do you know if the company who did the repair in the seventies still exists?"

"Nope. I presided over Old Tom's funeral myself six, no, seven, years ago. Why?"

"I hoped to look at records of the original repair. Sketches, glass sources, notes, anything that could help me."

"I may have something down in the catacombs. I tend to save everything. My daughter-in-law threatens to give my name to some TV show where they feature people who keep everything."

"This church has catacombs?"

"My daughter-in-law, Roberta, named them that, but as there are no bodies down there, I don't think they qualify. Think of them more as a low-ceilinged cellar with lots of partitions. Only the ones along the east wall are used for storage, as the ones on the west tend to seep during the spring. I haven't been down there for years."

"Would you mind if I look?"

"As long as you don't disturb anything. Sean tried to organize down there. But he gave up—too much junk. Do you know if he made his train?"

Tessa shrugged her shoulders. It would serve him right if he did miss it. First, being all flirtatious and then accusing her of what? Being nice? Why couldn't she ignore men like Candace the queen of never getting too involved?

The reverend stood. "Why don't we get a bite of lunch, and then I'll send you down to the catacombs. Don't forget to take an extra flashlight. The lights down there are not very reliable."

Tessa followed Reverend Cavanagh out the back door to a little two-story stone house. They entered through the kitchen door.

"My housekeeper is forever making too much food. She forgets it is only me. Sean comes by a couple times a week, but he mostly stays in the city." He opened an old museum-quality Westinghouse refrigerator. "Tuna salad and green Jell-O?" He made a face. "Probably the no-sugar kind, too. I keep telling her this stuff is for hospitals. There should be some bread in the keeper if you want a sandwich. Will you get me a slice of rye?"

Tessa sat across from Reverend Cavanagh as he said the prayer. It was one of the longest prayers she ever heard. By the time he finished, she was sure he'd blessed most of the residents in town with everything from help with a case of bursitis to some kid's college entrance exams. The only thing he was vague about was "a miracle for Sean." The reverend even prayed for her and the window. Tessa didn't think anyone but her grandmother ever prayed for her.

"So, tell me truthfully, were you expecting to be paid for fixing our window?"

Tessa squirmed. "My fee had never really been discussed. Mr. Beaufontaine left the details out when he emailed me. Since you arranged a place for me to stay, I am fine with the arrangement."

"But you would have liked to be paid."

"I won't lie. I'm a college student, so, of course, I would have liked to be paid." Seeing she was about to be interrupted, Tessa held up a hand. "But after seeing the window, it seems fixing it is the Christmassy thing to do. I mean, this town is so full of cheer and tinsel, fixing this window seems like a part of it." Tessa took a bite of her salad before she was overcome entirely by nostalgia. She sounded like a Homefire movie. But the town did look like one of the shows trademark Christmas sets.

"I am glad you are willing to do this. Will you be able to stay for our Christmas Eve service?"

"No, I need to leave no later than the twenty-third to get to my grandmother's in Connecticut. I should finish before then. The hardest thing is going to be finding glass. There is a twelve-inch square area needing to be completely rebuilt. When you cleaned up, you didn't happen to save the shards, did you?"

"As a matter of fact, I did. I put them in a shoe box. I wonder what I did with the box."

"Catacombs" was a perfect description for the cellar of the church. The number of boxes was overwhelming. It took Tessa only a few tries to realize the labels were not always accurate. Some items had been reboxed in plastic banker's bins. These were marked accurately. Unfortunately, they only represented the last twenty years. A quick perusal of the several storage rooms showed decades and even centuries worth of memorabilia stacked next to each other. She discovered that 82 might be 1982 or 1882. The only thing she found in meticulous order were the ledgers recording deaths, births, and marriages, which were lined up on a shelf in the first room.

Two long boxes with shipping labels to someplace in Ohio sat on the only table not covered in dust. Curiosity got the best of her.

Organ pipes. Why on earth would they be here? A note was attached inside of the eight-foot-long box.

Please repair in time for Christmas. I am quite sure the reeds need to be replaced in at least two. And, yes, I was insane enough to attempt the repair myself.

Sincerely,
Sean Cavanagh

She read the date. Two weeks ago. Why hadn't he sent them?

Closing the lid, she searched for an answer. On the corner of the table sat a blue shoe box. She didn't need to look inside to know the window shards would be in the box.

Could it be that the church was so short on funds they couldn't afford to repair both?

She pulled out her phone to search the cost of repairing organ pipes only to find the catacombs lacking in cell service. She'd check later.

Tessa continued her search of the older boxes and found a flyer from a victory dance from November 1918. She held the nearly century-old pamphlet and let her imagination run away with her. She could picture some girl getting her first kiss after the dance to celebrate the war to end all wars only to have her son be sent off to the Second World War when he turned twenty. If people knew how much pain lay ahead of them, would they still have fallen in love?

She put the paper back and moved on to the next box. Dog-eared copies of Handel's *Messiah*. From the dust on the box, it was obvious they hadn't been used for at least a decade. When she was twelve, her grandma had taken her to a sing-along presentation of the famous oratorio. She wondered if the church still had a choir to sing it or if that too had gone by the wayside.

An hour later she'd visited almost every decade but the seventies. It was hard to stay on task surrounded by so much history. She read the sermon given the Sunday after JFK was shot, and was reduced to tears. One box must have served as a lost and found from when women wore white gloves. Not one of the three matched, but the one with mother-of-pearl buttons fit perfectly.

Suddenly the lights flickered, then went out. A bit late to remember the warning to bring a flashlight. Fortunately she had her phone.

She met the reverend at the top of the stairs.

"Lights are out up here, too. I am going to check the fuse box."

Tessa followed him and was somewhat surprised to find the box was not one of the old types where you had to stick pennies over the fuse to get it to work. The sun was setting; she had no idea she had been downstairs so long. "Look, the rest of the block is dark too."

21

Reverend Cavanagh closed the breaker box. "Well, they finally did it—put up so many lights on the square they shut down the entire town. Let's go light some candles."

Tessa followed him into the sanctuary.

"One advantage of being a church—I always have candles."

Tessa heard the strike of a match as a tiny light sprung to life.

The reverend shook out the match after lighting five candles. "I often wonder what it was like in here 180 years ago. Was the building as drafty then? How did the congregations share it? Morning Mass and evening worship, I assume. When they built this place, did they stay on their own sides, or did the Italians help the Irish? Most of the information we have of those years is from stories passed down, and even those are dying."

For a moment he seemed lost somewhere in the past. He gave a sigh and shuffled to the first pew. "Did you find what you needed down there?"

"I found some wonderful things but not anything about the old window repair. I did find the window shards as well as some pipes to the organ."

"Yes, Sean repairs and tunes organs. He has been keeping this one in shape since he was a teenager. But this time he tells me there is something he can't fix. Now he says the organ won't work right for our Christmas Eve performance. He doesn't have enough faith. The music always comes. But he doesn't believe in miracles."

Tessa wasn't sure she believed in them either. Was there a way to get the pipes repaired in time? She hated to ask Mandy, but none of her other friends had an excess of money. Maybe it wasn't as expensive as she thought. If only she could figure out a way to save money on the window without sacrificing quality. She realized the reverend was asking her a question. Had he been talking the whole time?

"I'm not sure," she said, shooting for a one-size-fits-all answer.

"Well, at least you admit it."

Admit what?

22

"Sean won't admit it, but he has been unsure since 9/11. I think he only comes to church to check on me."

Okay, the conversation must be something about religion.

He reached over and gave her a grandfatherly pat on the arm. "Someday you will find your faith."

The light in the corridor flickered on. "Would you mind extinguishing the candles? I was going to get you a key to the back door. I am not always around, and Sean only pops in for Sunday service and when he is between jobs. This close to Christmas, he is busy. Everyone suddenly realizes their organ has dead notes. Now, me, I have known for six months we had dead notes." He shrugged before disappearing into his office.

He came back with a key attached to an iron candy cane–shaped ring. What was it with these large key rings? "Stay as long as you need to. Lock the back door on your way out. Leave the corridor light and the one by the front door on."

After he left, Tessa couldn't help but wonder how many ghosts lived in the old church.

Cobwebs. Sean cleaned another one off before moving forward. At least he hadn't found any rat droppings yet. But with an organ this dirty, it was no wonder they had enough ciphers to play a short requiem by turning the organ on. It wasn't unusual for an organ to get cipher notes—ones that seemingly played on their own when dirt lodged in a pipe valve, preventing it from closing. But the organ in this Bronx church was dirtier than most. Even if he fixed the known problematic pipes, there was no guarantee there wouldn't be more by Sunday.

The rector would not be pleased, but Sean hadn't scheduled the days of work this organ needed. Of the few pneumatics he inspected, nearly half had leather that needed to be replaced. Those were not helping with the sound quality either.

Sean crawled out of the chamber and went in search of the rector. He found him in the kitchen, nursing a cup of coffee.

"My goodness, you are filthy! Don't come in here! Are those cobwebs?" The little man shooed him back into the hallway. "So, are you done already?"

Sean counted to three before answering. "When was the last time the organ was serviced?"

"I'm not sure. Maybe about the time *Hamilton* debuted on Broadway."

"Two or three years?"

"Sounds about right."

Sean took a calming breath. "Did the last person to work on your organ tell you it would need to be tuned again in about six months?"

"Oh, you are one of those." The rector wiped the crumbs from his face with a napkin.

"One of what?"

"Repairmen who want to bilk the church out of money on a regular basis."

"No, I am not one of those. I am the kind who hates seeing a fine instrument like this perish due to neglect. I can fix and clean the pipes you know are playing randomly today, but the chamber is so dirty I can guarantee you will hear new ones by Christmas. I need a week inside her."

"Her?"

"Your organ. Most organs are temperamental and need a lot of TLC, like a woman. The point is, I can fix the immediate problems, but it is only a bandage."

"How much will this cost?"

Sean quoted two prices—one for the short-term fix and one for a complete overhaul.

The rector's eyes grew round. "I don't believe it!"

"The price is exclusive of having to send pipes out for repair."

"You mean you can't do it all?"

"Sometimes a repair requires specialized tools and fairly large equipment for the metal work. So, yes, some types of repairs are sent out."

"I still don't believe it."

"The price you would have paid for semiannual tunings during the last two years would have been much less. It is a true case of 'an ounce of prevention.' It is an old organ, so things would still need to be repaired, the leather on the pneumatics will still dry out and crack and many other age related repairs will be needed. But neglecting this old lady has only multiplied her problems. Look, I am willing to do what I can now, but I can't guarantee there won't be new problems in a week."

"You are saying if I did regular tunings, I wouldn't have any problems?"

"You would have some from time to time; after all, your organ isn't as young as she used to be. And even well-cared-for organs develop unforeseen issues."

"Like what?"

Sean searched for a story. "An example is the organ at one of the large, old theaters down in the city. One day the organist turned the Wurlizter on, and every pipe played at once. It was enough to practically deafen everyone in the building. An anomaly, I assure you, but things happen to huge machines."

"So, when could you do this overhaul?"

Sean checked the calendar on his phone. "The last week of January."

"I'll get back to you."

Sean left the building shaking his head. The little man wouldn't call him back and was probably negotiating with some novice repairman to do the job for less at this very moment. Sean looked up his next appointment. Hopefully they wouldn't mind him coming a day early. Maybe he could carve out a few more hours on his grandfather's organ this week.

five

THE WI-FI SIGNAL IN HER room faded into nonexistence again. Tessa took her tablet down to the lobby to do her research. She spent some time looking for photos of the Nativity window. Several tourist blogs contained some relatively decent images, but most of them focused on the faces. She found a couple with angles of the most damaged portion. What she really needed was the rubbings. Knowing where the lead lines should be in the section would save so much time.

Tessa found the organ repair shop online, but no prices were listed. Like her field, pipe fixing, or whatever it was called, must depend on the type of pipe and the difficulty of repair needed to be done. She broadened her search, hoping to find a ballpark estimate. After several searches, she finally got a figure from a European manufacturer.

Tessa covered her mouth when she realized she had gasped audibly.

"Is something wrong?" asked a gentleman in a business suit standing nearby.

"Yes—I mean no. Sorry. The numbers surprised me."

"Anything I can help with?"

Tessa shook her head. "No, I am trying to figure out how to do the impossible with nothing."

"Now that does sound interesting." The man sat down in the chair next to her. "How does one accomplish such a feat?"

"I wish I knew." Tessa wasn't sure how to get out of the conversation.

"People say I have a few good ideas from time to time. Maybe we could brainstorm." He gave Tessa one of those smiles she felt she could trust.

"All right. I am here to repair the window over at the church. I'm looking for some information on the last repair, which I can't find, but that's another problem. Anyway, I found two long boxes full of the trumpet pipes to the organ, which were meant to be sent out for repairs—only the window got broken, and it looks like they diverted the funds meant to repair the organ to repair the window. I want to figure out if there is a way to do both. I don't even know if there is time to get the pipes fixed."

"Where did you find them?" The man stroked his well-trimmed beard.

"Down in the catacombs on a long table."

"I used to play hide-and-seek down there as a boy." The man leaned back in his seat. "I assume the repair must be beyond what Sean Cavanagh can do."

Tessa didn't feel she should disclose the contents of the note as this person apparently knew Sean. "I believe so. I do have a friend I could ask to donate to the church, but I really don't want to run to her and her husband over this."

"Do you think they would help?"

"Maybe. She was my roommate for two years. I don't want to go begging because she married into money. It feels like I would be using them."

"Well, there is always a letter to Santa," he said with a wink.

She couldn't help but laugh in response. "Maybe the elves know how to repair organ pipes. I hadn't thought of the Santa option."

Two other men in business suits entered the lobby. The man who spoke to her stood. "Best of luck to you."

Tessa sat in the empty lobby and pondered what to say in a text to Mandy since a letter to Santa was doomed to failure.

six

TESSA SLIPPED THE KEY INTO the old doorknob as the sun crested the horizon. She'd opted to walk the four blocks to the church to clear her mind. The text to Mandy remained unsent.

She removed her coat but kept on her hoodie. Apparently they kept the building warm enough to keep the pipes in the addition containing the office and bathrooms from freezing. The chapel had been built long before central heating, but cast-iron radiators had been added near the turn of the century. During a full service, the building might be warm enough. Tessa thought she could see her own breath, but it might be her imagination.

The first thing she needed to do was to remove the duct tape, but that required a ladder. She found a four-foot step stool in a closet, along with a bucket and mop. An old drop cloth on a high shelf caught her eye. Using the mop handle, she pulled it off the shelf. She wouldn't be using a soldering iron today, so using the flammable cloth to catch any glass shards she missed would be safe enough.

The first piece of duct tape lifted easily, leaving minimal residue on the larger pieces of glass. However, it was reluctant to release the shards.

With the tape gone, the damage didn't look quite as bad. The first piece might be salvaged by using a copper-foiling technique.

The back door opened and shut. It must be the reverend. Tessa used tweezers to pull back the corner of the next piece.

"Excuse me."

Tessa turned and nearly lost her footing. The man from the hotel lobby stood a few feet away.

"Sorry, didn't mean to startle you. Have you seen Reverend Cavanagh this morning?"

"Sorry, no. I heard the back door open awhile ago."

"Probably me. His office is still locked."

"Sorry, can I help you?" The reverend hadn't told her what to do about people wandering into the church.

The man shook his head. "No, I'll come back later. Is that as tedious as it looks?"

"No. I mean, probably. I don't want to cause new damage by removing the tape, so I am going as slowly as I can. Should I tell the reverend you came by?"

"No, I'll find him later. Have a good day. I don't think I caught your name."

"Tessa, and you are?"

"Nick." He turned to leave, then paused. "Did you solve your organ problem yet? I mean, ask your friend for a donation?"

"No, I am hoping I don't need as much replacement glass as I thought. That would save some money and—" Tessa realized she was babbling. She wasn't sure why. The man looked nice enough, but he didn't have the presence Sean did. Not that Sean... Whatever. She let whatever she was going to say go. "You sure you don't want me to deliver a message?"

"No. I'll try to come by this afternoon, or early tomorrow morning. Bye, Tessa."

After he left, Tessa found herself comparing Nick to Sean. They were about the same age and of the same physical build. Considering her disastrous romance last spring with Gavin, she wondered what attracted her to one man over another. Nick was well-spoken, well-groomed, and, from the cut of the wool coat he wore over his suit, probably well-heeled, too. Yet nothing. No heart flutter, only her babbling, but that happened whenever she was nervous, not just around men. Sean, on the other hand, was a tad bit scruffy, but not deliberately so. His clothing showed he wasn't afraid to work hard but took care of himself. Thinking of him made her traitorous heart beat ever so slightly faster. Beards were not her thing, but Nick's seemed like it belonged. It wasn't like the ones the Hollywood actors wore because they were 'in.'

Tessa frowned. This would not do at all. She'd agreed with Candace—no more men this year. Only eighteen more days to go. She could do this. She opened the music app on her phone and selected a Christmas medley since some of her preferred playlists were probably not appropriate in a church.

Sean let the last note of Richard Elliott's *I Saw Three Ships* hang in the air. He loved this organ. It was one of the first he'd tuned when he'd started out. The organist had done her best to document any problems and to get the major ones fixed promptly. He should ask her to lecture the rector at the Bronx church he'd visited yesterday. That would be one mighty sermon.

He presented his bill at the office, almost half his bid since the organ didn't need another hour and a half worth of work, and he was surprised when the secretary paid him the original bid plus a bonus.

"This is too much."

"Consider it a Christmas bonus. You fit us in your schedule at the last minute. And if Mrs. Rodgers is happy with the organ, we are all happy.

Sean left the church whistling the refrain of *Wenceslas*. 4:10. He couldn't fit in another organ tonight. Too many were in churches that held a Wednesday-night service or choir practice anyway. He turned his car to head out of town. Might as well check on Granda.

Once he crossed the river and headed north, he let his mind drift to Tessa. She'd invaded his thoughts all day. His earlier rudeness bothered him. She probably felt something like he did when the rector had questioned his motives for wanting to service the Bronx organ on a more regular basis. He owed her an apology.

But that was all. As much as Granda wished it, Sean never would "get serious" with a girl again. He'd made a vow and intended to keep it.

seven

THE LAST ROOM. UNLESS TESSA was lost in the catacombs, this was the last room containing any boxes. She'd saved it for last because it was the most jumbled. She forced herself to skim through any boxes not from the 1970s, looking only for rolled papers, as the window could have been documented earlier.

Dust tickled her nose, and she sneezed.

"Dia linn." Where had Sean come from?

Tessa dug for a tissue in her pocket. "What did you say?"

"Dia linn. It is an Irish form of 'Bless you.'"

"Oh, thank you."

"Have you seen my boxes?"

Tessa waved at the dozens surrounding her. "Any in particular? I am not entirely sure, but Indiana Jones could have hidden the Ark down here."

Sean smiled.

Tessa willed her heart to slow down. She'd analyzed the likelihood of a relationship with the attractive man, and it was pointless.

"If the Ark is here, it's safe. No, these were long boxes about eight feet and heavy." Sean used his arms to show the size of the boxes.

"The ones with the organ pipes in them? They were in room four on a table."

"You numbered the rooms?"

Tessa consulted the sketch she'd made in her little book. "Yes, I wanted to make sure I didn't miss anything. There are such fantastic treasures down here. I have been listing them. Some of them should be in a museum. Do you have a local history museum?" She clamped her jaw shut. She was babbling again. Had the room grown a little warmer?

"You're sure the pipe boxes were there?" Sean pointed the direction of the room the boxes had been.

Tessa read the book again. "Yes, room four is the only one with a long table. Six has a table, but it rocks. I am not sure a hymnal should be used to steady it."

"When did you see the boxes last?" Sean studied the room she was in as if hoping the boxes would suddenly appear.

"Yesterday afternoon before the power outage."

"Are you sure?"

"Of course. Have I given you some reason to doubt me?" Tessa did not want to go back to where they'd left off yesterday morning.

Sean studied his shoes for a moment. "Sorry, I didn't mean to accuse you, but the boxes are missing, and I know Granda isn't strong enough to move them."

"Missing?" Tessa slipped past Sean and hurried to the room. As indicated, the boxes were gone. She ran her hand over the empty place.

"Now who is doubting who?" A smile colored his voice.

"They were here yesterday. I promise. I looked in the boxes, but I didn't touch them. I haven't heard anyone else down here all day."

"Not very reassuring. You didn't hear me come down over your music, either."

"It wasn't that loud."

"But your singing was."

"I don't sing."

Sean was polite enough to answer with a smile. "You are not bad,

36

but you are a natural alto; trying to sing soprano is your problem."

"An alto? Aren't they the ones who get all the boring parts?"

"On the contrary. They can sing very nice parts. Cher, Judy Garland, and Karen Carpenter are examples of famous altos."

"So is that why I think I sound decent when I sing 'Have Yourself a Merry Little Christmas'?" Tessa moved to put the table between them. She'd promised Candace no holiday romances, but when Sean smiled, she wanted to text her friend and tell her the deal was off. It was much easier to keep her promise when he growled.

"What are you searching for anyway?"

"A rubbing or, even more impossibly, the original plan for the windows. Some of the came was bent and twisted, and I don't know the original shape of the glass. I haven't tried piecing together the shards, but if I can't find the plans, I may end up trying that next."

"*Came*? Don't you mean *cane*?"

"Nope, it is *came*, with an *m*. Remember my explanation the other day?" Tessa moved back to the last room and opened another box.

Sean followed. "I've looked in most of the boxes at some point. What would a rubbing look like?"

"Both the plan and the rubbing would be rolled up and the size of the window. I am also looking for receipts for the repair done in the seventies. I want to know what glass house they used. I am fairly sure the blue uses a cobalt recipe banned by the EPA. Trying to find a close match is going to be very difficult, and if I can find a hundred-year-old piece of glass, the process may have been similar."

"Like finding matching ivory to repair an old keyboard. Not only is ivory illegal to sell, but the quality of what comes from old keyboards also varies so much. It is easier to use high-quality plastic replacements." Sean opened the box nearest him.

"I've already finished that stack. I believe you are looking at flannel-board Bible stories."

"How did you remember what was in this box? It looks like so many of the others."

"I have a partially photographic memory. I can't remember words for the life of me, but shapes, pictures, items in a box—those I can recall fairly consistently."

"Amazing."

"Or annoying. Depends on your point of view. My roommates get annoyed when I can recall every painting I ever studied. I get annoyed as sometimes I see the picture of the frog from my ninth-grade biology class textbook when I am trying to fall asleep." Tessa closed a box of fabric.

Sean opened another box. "I owe you an apology. I was rude yesterday when I questioned your motives. Don't get me wrong. I am glad you are fixing the window, and it fits in Granda's budget, but—"

"But you budgeted the money to fix the trumpet pipes, right?"

"How did you know?"

"Once I found the boxes, I put two and two together and did a search. Even if I can keep this job under $1,000 in materials, which, with the new protective window probably won't happen, there isn't the $4,000 or $5,000 you need for the pipes, is there?"

Sean shook his head. "I planned to revive Handel's *Messiah* this year to surprise Granda. I've been working with the choirs from the other churches around here. And I really need those pipes."

"And now they are missing." Tessa closed the last box. "As is any trace of the repair of the seventies."

"Maybe not." Sean held up a baseball. "It is signed July 2, 1979, by my father, Cameron. The other side is signed by Ansley Gooding."

Tessa hurried over to look in the box. "Receipts!" She took a handful and moved directly below the bare lightbulb.

"Anything?"

"No and yes. I have the name of where they got the glass, but I am pretty sure they went out of business a decade ago. But the receipt is for more glass than could have been used. You haven't seen a box of glass anywhere?"

"Sorry, no."

The lights flickered and dimmed.

"Not again." Tessa pulled out her phone and fumbled for the flashlight app.

Across the room, a flashlight sprang to life. "Did this happen last night?"

"Yes, the power was out for several blocks."

Sean held out his hand. "Come on, let's go check the fuse box. I doubt there is a second outage."

His hand was firm and slightly calloused. Tessa knew if there were ghosts in the catacombs, Sean could keep them away.

"My bag. Shine a light over here so I can gather my things." When she finished, Tessa set her hand back in his.

It felt too perfect there. It wasn't wimpy, like she was trying too hard to rely on him. It fit like a reed pipe fit its base. They wound their way through the rooms until they reached the bottom of the stairs, where light filtered down the stairway from above.

"Looks like the basement blew a fuse." Sean kept hold of her hand as they climbed. Once they were in the corridor, he reluctantly let go, wishing he had an excuse to hold it a moment more.

Granda was already at the fuse box. "Did you find anything down there?"

Tessa answered. "Maybe. Do you remember there being any glass left over from the repair in '75?"

"Can't say I do, but then, I tend to forget more than I remember most days. There. That should do it. Sean, go make sure those lights are off."

It wasn't until Sean reached the bottom of the stairs that he wondered if Granda might have thrown the switch. "No more matchmaking," Sean muttered as he went from room to room, pulling the chains hanging from the lights. Sean didn't do love. He'd watched his mother lose his father, and it had nearly killed her. He'd seen Granda's loneliness since his grandmother passed. Sean wasn't above an occasional fling with someone he met at a nightclub, but it never lasted. Tessa didn't seem like the type who was in town for some two-week romance. And he was tired of those, too.

eight

O'MALLEY'S WAS NOT WHAT SHE expected. But then, she had never been in an Irish pub before. Tessa still wasn't sure how she'd ended up there with Sean. When they'd left the church, there had been three of them. At some point halfway across the square, the reverend vanished. Of course, almost everyone they passed had stopped the old clergyman to show him some preparation for the festival starting tomorrow. The town only needed a dusting of snow to be Homefire perfect. A camera crew had been filming over by the gazebo, probably recording some feelgood news story.

A red-haired man hailed them from behind the bar. "Sean, m'lad. W'ere ya bin?"

Sean turned to Tessa. "Don't believe a word Mike says. The accent is as fake as his red hair."

"M'hair is all natural. It says so on the bottle. Who's this? And what lies did ye tell 'er to get 'er to go to dinner with ya?"

Sean dropped a protective arm around Tessa's shoulders. Automatically she stepped into his side. Mike wasn't threatening, but she felt he might try to turn on his best Don Juan given the chance. "This is Tessa Doyle. She's here to fix the window." Sean looked down at Tessa. "This charlatan is Michael O'Malley. His younger brother *used* to own a drone."

Tessa studied the proprietor. He was dressed like an overgrown leprechaun, complete with green bow tie and gold vest. She thought of the teen at the inn. Sean must be correct about the source of the red hair.

"And me accent comes naturally. The day I kissed the ol' stone." He made a kissing noise for emphasis.

"There is a reason they call it the Blarney stone." Sean's voice was low enough she was sure the comment was meant for her ears only.

Tessa was tempted to laugh at both men. "Odd. I kissed it and *my* voice didn't change."

"And wee lovely voice it is, too. But yer not Irish, are ya? You be Norse?"

"Swedish."

"See, the stone only works on those born with Gaelic blood!" The last sentence contained only a hint of an accent.

Sean consulted his watch and shook his head. "Not even three minutes. There is no way you can keep your accent going all weekend."

"Can't blame me for trying. I had the California film crew going at lunch. I think they were fooled."

"Film crew?"

"Yeah, someone thinks our little Christmas festival is the perfect backdrop for one of those lovey-dovey chick flick Christmas movies." Michael rolled his eyes. "Find yourselves a seat. Special is the Shepherd's Pie." He waved them off.

Sean dropped his arm. "Booth or table?"

"I don't care, as long as it is not under one of the TVs." There were few things Tessa hated more than being in a restaurant with a guy who was so interested in the sport being played overhead he couldn't carry on a thirty-second conversation unless a commercial played. "Will your grandfather be joining us?"

They picked a booth by the back wall.

"Maybe. If he doesn't, I'll order him some carryout."

Sean didn't bother opening his menu before the waitress took his order. Tessa tried the special.

Dinner was fun. With the intensity of a real fan, Sean explained why the Mets were a better team than the Yankees. Tessa still pictured the museum every time he said the word *Met*. Confessing such nearly left her paying for both dinners. Then the subject changed to music, more specifically organs.

"Last year I cleaned and tuned more than three hundred organs, not including Granda's. I started cleaning it when I was thirteen or so and got ahold of a how-to book. I was lucky I didn't cause any more damage than I did."

"Part of me is surprised there are so many organs around, but I guess this is the Big Apple. If I was looking for a place to exclusively restore windows, New York would be in the top ten."

"You mean that's not what you want to do?"

Tessa took another bite before answering. "I want to create them. I practically completed my MFA project before I earned my BFA. Only second semester student in the history of the school to display their show before completing the last year."

"But I thought you needed this window for your MFA. If your project is done, why?"

"I chose to do a practical application, for lack of better term, as part of my study. I spent January to May in Europe learning glass-preservation and repair techniques. To get credit, I needed 160 hours of repairing and documenting windows. I came back from Europe about twenty hours shy. The Nativity window is at least forty hours of work, so I should finish off the course."

"What else do you need to graduate?"

"Basically write a few papers, show a PowerPoint to the faculty. I don't even need to go full-time next semester as I only register for my review class. I taught last semester, but I've thought of trying to get a commission to build something for a real client. Candace says I can clean out the garage and use it for a studio."

"Who's Candace?"

How did one describe the best roommate ever? Tessa managed it, from the activities of the Friday Night Artist Society and their incredibly painted house to the various wigs Candace wore.

"Why wear so many wigs?"

Tessa shook her head. "Only Candace can tell you that."

"You don't know?"

"Of course I know, but it is her story. She decides who she wants to tell and who she wants to leave guessing."

"But I'll likely never meet her."

Tessa shrugged. "Then it will be one of life's mysteries."

For a moment she thought Sean might not let it go, but his phone beeped.

Halfway through dinner, Sean received a text from Granda: **The Sullivans asked me to dinner. Sorry for leaving you ;)**

Sean wondered if the winky-face emoji wasn't an indication of Granda's matchmaking. Although the dinner conversation had been pleasant, it stayed on safe and generic topics. Tessa was as guarded as he was.

It wasn't often he dined with a female who didn't seem to want something more from him.

The waitress brought the check.

"Did you drive to the church this morning? I don't recall seeing an extra car behind the church."

Tessa looked up from searching in her bag. "No, I walked." She pulled out a twenty. "This should cover—"

Sean held up his hand. "Granda would have my head if I let you pay for dinner. Consider it my treat—the least I can do after questioning your motives yesterday."

"You don't need to, but I am not going to pass up a free meal, either. Next one is on me." She slipped the money back into her bag.

No chance of that happening. But Sean knew better than to argue. "Come on, I'll walk you to the hotel."

"I thought you wanted to get some practice on the organ tonight."

"I'll have enough time to practice, and you will be saving me a lecture from Granda on my generation not having any manners."

"Well, if you are going to put it that way, I'll save you the lecture." She stood and picked her jacket up off the bench.

Without thinking, Sean took it from her and helped her get it on the same way his father always helped his mother. When he was finished, Tessa turned to him.

"Wow, if your grandfather does give you a lecture, I'll inform him it is not needed. I don't think anyone has helped me with my coat since I was five."

"I didn't mean to embarrass you. My father always did that, and I guess I've made it a habit in his honor."

"You didn't embarrass me." Tessa's cheeks pinked. "It isn't often I experience manners out of old Cary Grant movies."

"Is that a comment on my age?"

The pink deepened. "No, I didn't—" She looked around the room, her cheeks taking on a glow not unlike the fabled reindeer's nose. Tessa continued in a quieter voice. "People are— We should—"

Determined now to put Cary Grant to shame, at least for the next ten minutes, Sean extended his arm. They made it out of O'Malley's before bursting into laughter. They stopped at the crosswalk. Sean took a little bow. "Alas, there is not a puddle, or I would put my coat down."

Tessa laughed harder. "You wouldn't!"

The crosswalk chime chirped. "But I would. Anything to make Granda believe all of my nana's lectures finally made it to my heart."

45

Lights flickered briefly on the huge pine in the center of the square.

"Another power outage?"

"No, they are doing a quick test before the lighting tomorrow night. Mr. Tanner believes in double-checking everything."

"It is a gorgeous tree. Where'd they get it?"

"Right here. It's been growing on the square for about fifty years."

"So it is live? Amazing."

"The entire town could run out of water, but we would still find a way to care for the three trees we use as the alternating center of the festival." Sean pointed to two other trees. "On hot days, kids will come poor cups of water on the roots after hearing from their grands that the trees must never die. We just don't tell them that about every seventeen years or so the oldest one is replaced by a new one."

"Did you water the trees when you were little?"

Sean nodded. "I did better than that. I stole ice from Nana's freezer."

They walked around the tree, Tessa's arm still linked through his. As they completed their circuit, a man rushed up to them. "Would you two help us? Some of the extras didn't show up tonight, and we need another couple to walk through the background of the scene we are shooting."

Sean noted the logo on the man's jacket—some cable channel, he thought.

The man turned to Sean. "All you need to do is keep escorting your girlfriend—"

"I'm not—"

"She's not—" they protested in unison.

The man waved his hand. "I don't care what you want to call it. I just want you to keep walking like you were and smiling at each other from time to time."

Tessa shook her head only a fraction of an inch.

Sean started to tell the man no.

"There is fifty in it for both of you for an hour of your time."

Tessa's hand tightened on Sean's arm. He raised his brows, hoping she understood the question. His answer was a tiny smile and a shrug.

He turned back to the man. "Sure. Why not?"

"Come with me. I have a couple of papers for you to sign, and makeup will want to check you." He walked off in the direction of a trailer parked at the far side of the gazebo.

THIS IS CRAZY." TESSA GLANCED up from the papers she was signing. "We're going to be extras in a Homefire Christmas movie." She couldn't wait to text Candace.

Sean met her eyes. "A bit more than crazy." She was afraid he was annoyed, then he smiled.

"This goes beyond good manners."

"Fifty dollars beyond. Plus, I can record it next year on Granda's DVR and freeze the frame we are in to prove I once had manners."

She laughed. "He'll tell you it doesn't count if you got paid."

"Wow, you already sound like him, and you have only been around him for two days."

Two women came over and told them to turn around. "Like the bag."

"Nice coloring," said the one examining Sean's face.

"Hat?"

One of them picked up a strand of Tessa's hair. "You owe me ten. She is a natural blonde."

The other produced a pale-blue knit hat and scarf. "Don't move, sweetie. I want to get this one right the first time."

Out of the corner of her eye, she saw the other woman pull out some makeup and a sponge, which she aimed at Sean's face. He stepped back.

"Oh, don't do that!" said the woman with the hat. "He has such a perfect shadow, and you don't want to color it. Put a bit of blush on her. "Sweetie, do you have any lipstick in that bag of yours?"

Tessa produced the lone tube of red.

The woman eyed it. "Not your shade, but you'll be in the background. Next time you shop, get something with a bit more rose in it." She proceeded to snatch the tube from Tessa's hand and apply it.

"Perfect. Now hurry on over to the gazebo."

Once they were alone, Sean leaned close. "Just so you know, if she had touched me with the makeup, I would have left."

"I wouldn't have blamed you."

The little man gave some general instructions, then paused to address them. "You are couple number three. Walk like you did around the tree. You are going to start up there." He pointed to where a young man with a tablet stood. "Walk when and where he tells you to."

"I guess we should go." Sean extended his arm.

The wind picked up a bit, and Sean shivered. He pulled Tessa closer to his side. "Are you warm enough?" They were on their fifth walk across the square.

Tessa leaned in. "As warm as I can be. But I think my smile may have frozen. Does it look unnatural?"

"When I was little, my mother would tell me not to stick out my tongue because my face would freeze that way. I didn't believe her. But now? Maybe."

"My mother said the same thing."

They reached the end of their guided walk. A person bundled

to Eskimo-like proportions holding a tablet looked up at them. "Okay, number three, this time you need to walk on this path and pass in front of the gazebo. He wants you to laugh. Tell each other corny jokes. It usually works. Boyfriend, you need to switch sides with her since she is shorter. On the count of ten, then go slowly."

They adjusted positions and started walking. "I can't come up with a single joke. Other than the knock-knock jokes we used earlier," said Sean.

"I have a ton of blonde jokes I've collected over the years."

One of Tessa's pale locks fell in her face. Sean was tempted to pull off his glove and touch it. Tessa brought her hand up, but Sean stopped her.

"Here, let me." He was careful not to touch her skin with the glove lest it scratch her. Her blue eyes followed his hand.

"Thanks."

Had he only imagined that her reply was a tiny bit breathless? They were taking this acting like a couple thing too far. "I think we are supposed to laugh."

"Okay, how do you keep a blonde in suspense?" Tessa grinned at him.

Sean shook his head. "I don't know."

"I'll tell you tomorrow."

"But I'm not—" Sean laughed, catching himself.

"That is one of my favorites as it gets everyone regardless of hair color."

"Remind me to try that one on O'Malley." Sean moved to the left to avoid a group of kids.

"Here is the next one. Why are blonde jokes so short?"

Sean was still contemplating an answer when the director yelled. "Couple three, stop right there and keep talking." Sean stopped, and Tessa turned to face him, her eyes questioning. Not sure if she was concerned about his lack of an answer or the change in their routine, he answered both. "I have no idea."

"So brunettes can remember them." Tessa smiled up at him.

"Couple number three, look up!"

Mistletoe.

Tessa's eyes grew wide, her mouth forming a silent O.

"Boyfriend number three, get on with it. You've wanted to all night!"

How did the director know? Sean started to lower his head and whispered, "Okay?"

Tessa moved her hands to his chest and looked from his eyes to his mouth and back again. Sean took that as permission. He hadn't done a stage kiss since the high school production of *Seven Brides for Seven Brothers*, an experience he'd tried hard to erase from his memory. This stage kiss accomplished his goal. Tessa leaned into him and kissed him back. She tasted like the cider from their last break. Mindful of the camera crew, he pulled back and gave Tessa a smile. Her blush deepened, but it could have been the cold.

"Couple three, proceed slowly along your route."

Sean tucked Tessa back in at his side and walked to the end of the path.

Neither spoke.

They were met by another crew member. "Wonderful job on the kiss—best one of the night. Go over to the trailer, turn in your props if you have any, and pick up your check. Good night, couple three."

At the trailer, Tessa turned in her knit hat and matching scarf. Her hair stood on end due to static. She tried unsuccessfully to smooth it.

Sean removed his scarf and wrapped it around her head, tying it under her chin. "There. That will keep you warm until we reach the inn." He took her hand and headed back out into the cold.

TESSA FLOPPED ON THE BED. What happened tonight was not just a stage kiss. Not that she'd ever tried drama, but she was pretty sure stage kisses didn't have the kind of chemistry she'd felt.

Sean hadn't mentioned a theatrical background, but he must have one. Either that or a lot more experience kissing than she assumed. Tessa would rather believe it was a theater background. It was the best explanation for a kiss that ... that—wow!

Tessa needed her roommates.

She texted Candace. **Help! I just received the most mind-blowing kiss ever!**

What? NO KISSING! Better than Gavin??

— Gavin who?

Calling!

Tessa didn't even get a chance to say hello before Candace started in. "Girl! What on earth? We agreed after you came home that there was no more kissing until next year."

"Well, I didn't plan on it. It was kind of a stage kiss, but it felt so real."

"Stage kiss?"

"Sean and I were asked to be extras for a Homefire movie."

"Whoa, back up here. Who is Sean, and how did you get into one of their movies?"

Tessa gave Candace a rundown of her week. "Then he walked me back to the inn. We only mentioned how cold it was. He left me at the door to the lobby; didn't even come in. I still have his scarf." Tessa picked it up. Oh, it smelled like him—a bit of spice, hard work, and maybe lemon?

"Girl, I know you are smelling his scarf. Put it down now. It is poison!"

"Candace, I am a mess. Why can't I ignore guys the way you do?"

"I don't ignore guys."

"Then what do you call what you did to Colin at Mandy's wedding?"

"I was busy. I wasn't ignoring him."

Tessa wrapped the scarf around her neck. "Whatever you call it."

"We are just friends. He was the best man, and I was the maid of honor. End of story."

It was wiser to keep her thoughts on the matter to herself. "So, what do I do with Sean?"

"Nothing. You will be gone in a week and a half. He wouldn't have kissed you if the director hadn't told him to, so don't make a big deal out of it. No more broken hearts. And no more kissing."

"You are right. I don't know much about him anyway, and he did jump to conclusions about my motives."

"Repeat after me. Long-distance relationships never work."

"Long-distance relationships never work because you don't know when he is cheating on you. Thanks, Candace." Tessa removed the scarf and folded it on the desk. "A magically devastating kiss is not a foundation for a relationship."

"Hugs, my friend. Text me a single S when you feel yourself slipping, and I'll call and rescue you."

"Night, Candace."

Sleep didn't come as quickly as she hoped it would. Tessa tried not to replay a kiss that could play next year in millions of living rooms across the country if it wasn't left on the cutting-room floor. She needed to remember the kiss was for a Homefire Christmas movie and real life was never as romantic as an iconic film.

Sean only turned on a couple of lights. Despite the hour, he still needed to practice. There had to be a way to play the "Hallelujah Chorus" without the trumpet pipes. At least they were only doing the first part of the *Messiah* and ending with the "Hallelujah Chorus" from the second part. The aria "The Trumpet Shall Sound" in the third part would be disastrous.

The missing pipes nettled him. Granda hadn't been down in the catacombs for years, and even if he did manage to get down the stairs without his cane, he didn't have the strength to lift the boxes. Tessa would need several trips to move them, but why would she? Sean doubted she knew the full significance of the pipes until their conversation. If she had played some kind of joke, she'd had more than enough time to confess.

After changing into his organ shoes and doing several run-throughs, trying various stops and combinations, Sean wasn't happy with the sound but hoped it would be passable with the choirs singing. If the organists were present at the three jobs he'd lined up for the rest of the week, he would see what they suggested.

He turned off the organ and put back on his tennis shoes. At least he didn't have any dead notes or ciphers. Granda's organ was probably the most babied in the entire state. Sean used the instrument as an excuse to come visit Granda on a regular basis. In the past five years, the old lady had reached a state of practically spotless glory. Sean thought his efforts were unmatched until a friend described his tour of the Salt Lake Tabernacle organ in Utah. The chambers of that organ approached an impossible level of operating-room cleanliness. Even if he worked for weeks, he would never have this old lady that clean. Dust had too many places to accumulate for one man to keep up with it.

His phone beeped a text message. His mom.

Are you still up?

— No, I'm sleep texting.

Very funny. I only wanted you to know my plans. My flight lands at midnight on the 22nd.

— Okay, I'll be there.

No need. Richard and I are renting a car.

Sean wasn't sure how to respond. He liked his mother's longtime boyfriend well enough, but it seemed that every time they came to New York together, his mom got all melancholy and ended the relationship.

— Are you staying at the apartment?

No, we have reservations at the Holiday Inn in Peekskill.

Better there than the apartment. He'd finally decided to do some updating and wasn't sure she would approve. If he'd had a chance of getting something else in the price range of his rent-controlled lease, Sean would have moved years ago. There were too many memories left there, and with the fire station so near, there were still days when the sound of the sirens from the station took him back to his childhood.

— Granda will be glad to have you here for Christmas Eve.

With the surprise you have planned, we wouldn't miss it. Can't believe you got the Messiah going again!

Sean didn't have the heart to tell Mom the concert might not be the way she remembered it. But then, nothing was as good as memories made it.

— See you next week. Love you.

Love you too.

Sean stared at his phone. He'd known Mom coming was a possibility, but it was Richard's daughter's year, wasn't it? But they'd gone on a cruise with Gail and her new husband this summer when Gail got married. Sean shivered. He was all for family togetherness, but having your father and his girlfriend on your honeymoon cruise was a bit too much togetherness.

He double-checked the locked door before crossing the yard to Granda's. The wind whistled through the belfry. Sean reached absentmindedly to adjust a scarf that wasn't there. Tessa. Just when he'd managed to go at least fifteen minutes without thinking about her.

eleven

As Tessa drove to the church, she hoped Sean had already left for the city. Then she could leave the scarf with the reverend. She wouldn't be long today anyway. She'd found two promising stained-glass suppliers in New Jersey and another in Brooklyn, which she'd rather avoid driving to.

Finding a piece of drapery glass to replace the broken part of Mary's dress was next to impossible. But there were also a few hothouses around. They might make her a small piece close to matching. Had she known the specifications of the break before driving out here from Indiana, she could have gone down to Kokomo Glass, where she'd worked the summer of her junior year. They had most likely poured the original glass if it was for Tiffany. But the church couldn't afford an entire crate of the custom glass, which would be the minimum order.

A regular piece of antique or semi-antique in matching blue would have to do. Maybe a Cobalt Opalume would work.

She also needed various supplies, including more lead came, a wax stone, and acid-free vellum—no way was she going to leave without documenting the window. There must be someplace she hadn't searched. Did the church have an attic? Probably not, with the vaulted ceiling.

Reverend Cavanagh was in the office when she arrived. "Morning, Tessa. You barely missed Sean."

Relief and disappointment clashed inside her. She laid the scarf over the back of the chair nearest the door. "Will you see that he gets this? We did miss you at dinner."

The old man chuckled. "I am sure you had more fun without me. Besides, no director wants an octogenarian reverend walking through their movie."

Tessa didn't want to know what he knew about last night. "Did you think of anyplace else I might find the rubbings?"

"Nick did ask me to think about donating some things to the new museum awhile ago. I sent over a few boxes. I'll call him and check."

"I do hope something is there. I am off to a couple of glass suppliers in New Jersey. I know we talked about my work, but we didn't cover the cost of supplies. As much as I would like to, I don't think I can donate them."

The reverend pulled out a twenty. "Here's something to help with gas money. Keep your receipts and invoice us. If you can keep it under $1,000, it would be helpful. Sean really wants to send out some parts of the organ to be fixed, and I am trying to have something in the budget."

Tessa took the gas money and slipped it in her pocket before running downstairs to wrap up several of the larger shards to take as a comparison.

She ran her hand over the empty table, then used her cellphone light to check in the first couple of catacombs for the missing pipes. Only dust. She didn't have time to look in all of them, and Sean probably already had. Hopefully the rest of her day wouldn't prove as futile.

Standing room only. The train out to Blue Pines was more crowded than Sean anticipated. He'd learned from experience that driving to Granda's during the Snowy Night festival was an exercise in frustration. Apparently he wasn't the only one to figure this out.

He shouldn't have come tonight, especially after the organ he'd worked on this afternoon needed more TLC than he'd counted on. He'd nearly worn out four one-dollar bills cleaning the reeds. With each one he cleaned, he thought about his own missing pipes. They had to be in the church someplace. Maybe some of the teens had gotten in and decided to play a joke by hiding things in the catacombs. Conducting a further search was his main reason to go to the church.

The fact that he was daydreaming of the world's favorite parasitic plant had nothing to do with anything. Mistletoe killed trees. What idiot had decided people should kiss under it?

"Next stop, Blue Pines. For all you festival attendees, remember the 10:08 is the last train back to the city tonight."

Sean joined the throng of passengers exiting the train, avoiding Main Street as he hurried to the parsonage. Granda had fallen asleep watching Perry Mason reruns. Sean left his pack in the bedroom that over the years had become his, ate some leftover casserole, and headed to the church.

Only the night safety lights were on. The protective board Tessa had placed over the window after removing the duct tape was still up. Had she wasted another day looking for the nonexistent papers? If she didn't get some work done soon, they wouldn't have a window or an organ for Christmas.

He grabbed the Maglite out of the closet, along with a piece of chalk. It was easy to get turned around in these empty chambers. Years ago he'd known every corner of the church, but he was in no mood to double back and repeat himself tonight because he'd forgotten which chambers dead-ended.

As expected, the majority of the rooms were empty. In the far southwest room was a wooden crate that had sat there so long the letters had faded to read "AG-LE." He'd climbed on the box more than once, trying to reach the small window above it. He marked the room with an *X* and moved on.

Scraping sounds echoed as he worked his way around the northwest corner rooms. He checked the time on his watch—a couple minutes past eight. No one should be in the building. Maybe his pipe thief had returned. Keeping his flashlight aimed at the floor, he walked toward the room Tessa called number seven. The light was off, but he could see a light on in one of the chambers ahead. He turned off his light and crept toward the intruder.

A kid in a hoodie stood with his back to him, fumbling with something at the table where his pipes had lain two days earlier.

"Hey! What are you doing?"

twelve

TESSA SCREAMED AS SHE GRABBED the huge candy-cane key ring and whirled around to defend herself. "Sean!"

"What are you doing here so late?" He folded his arms and leaned against the doorway, the skeptical look from the day they met having returned.

Dropping the key ring to her side, Tessa took a steadying breath before answering. "I was bringing down the supplies I purchased today."

"It took you all day to get supplies?"

"In case you haven't noticed, Blue Pines doesn't exactly have an opalescent glass warehouse. So I drove to New Jersey, where I was moderately successful at one of the two suppliers I found there. I never did locate one of the addresses in Brooklyn, but I did find a hot shop. Unfortunately, they will charge over $400 to custom-make the broken piece of Mary's dress, so I did not commission it. Then I drove back here. I have been on the road for the past three hours without a bathroom or food. But my priority was to make sure the glass made it safely, as I purchased nearly $800 worth since the store will let me return any uncut and undamaged glass in the next seven days. Now, if you have enough information, I am going to go get my other box and find the restroom." Tessa ran upstairs and straight to the bathroom. The day had been beyond frustrating. New York prices! The last thing she needed was Sean cross-examining her as if she were some criminal.

After washing her hands, she turned the water to cold and splashed her face. Had she just lectured Sean? He wasn't going to know she was falling apart. She patted her face dry, straightened her shoulders, and left the restroom.

Sean stood in the corridor, the bags from her car in one hand and her purse over his shoulder. He held out her keys. "I locked your car and took out your purse. There are a lot of people wandering about out there. Most of them are probably honest, but there are probably a few pickpockets too."

Tessa removed her bag from his shoulder. "Thank you. I should have thought about that. I have my phone in my pocket, and I was so worried about the glass." She reached for the other bags, but Sean started walking toward the stairs. She followed.

When they reached storeroom number four, he set them on the table and turned to face her. "Sorry I scared you. After seeing the addresses on these bags, I am surprised you made it back before morning." He offered an apologetic smile.

"Sorry I snapped. It hasn't been the best of days, and I nearly ended it with a heart attack." Tessa started to pull out several items. "Do you know where I might find a floor lamp or some other light source? I've found this is the best place to work on the pane I am going to remove, but the lighting is dismal." A light box was too much to ask for, and she didn't want to explain the purpose of one. Maybe the hardware store would have something she could rig. A large picture frame with its protective glass over a table lamp could work in a pinch.

"You can't do it while it is in the window?"

"Only some of the repairs can be done in the vertical window. The most damaged section is in one of the smaller side frames. There is so much work to be done, it is much easier to do it when it is lying down." Tessa kept rearranging items so she didn't need to look at Sean. Her stomach growled.

"Do you like cinnamon rolls?"

"What?" His brown eyes crinkled at the corners when he smiled.

"Cinnamon rolls. Wait here, and I'll go get…" He finished the sentence as he ran up the stairs.

After sorting her purchases, there was nothing else Tessa could do tonight. She turned out the storeroom light and hoped whoever took the pipes left the glass alone.

She'd just reached the top of the stairs when Sean came in through the back door balancing two Styrofoam mugs and a paper sack.

"I guarantee these are the best cinnamon rolls in the world."

Tessa reached for one of the cups. Mmmm—hot chocolate.

"Is that the only jacket you own?"

"No, I have my heavy coat in the car."

"Just a minute. Let me see what Granda has in his office." Sean set the bag and his cup down on a small table and disappeared. He came back with a heavy wool coat over his arm and his scarf around his neck. "Thanks for returning this. Put on the coat. I want to show you something. And grab your cup." Sean led her to the little closet in the entryway of the church and unlocked it.

A wrought-iron staircase circled up.

"Are you afraid of heights or claustrophobic?" Sean held open the door.

"No, neither."

"Good. Can you balance your cup?"

"I've had a bit of practice on this type of staircase. If the lid stays on, I'll be fine." Tessa followed Sean up the dizzying stairs.

They passed a little door in the wall and kept going. At the top, Sean stopped and lifted a hatch-type door. The silhouette of the bell stood out against the starry sky. He set his cup and bag down and turned to help her in the cramped space. Sean maneuvered her into the corner and then shut the door.

"Careful of the bell. It isn't supposed to ring until Christmas Eve."

"Only one day a year?"

"Three. Christmas Eve, Christmas Day, and New Year's. It also rings the first Monday of December at noon while the other bells are ringing, to test it. But everyone pretends they don't hear it."

Tessa smiled and sipped her hot chocolate and looked out at the city. "I hadn't realized there were so many Christmas lights up. But why isn't the tree lit?"

"They don't light it until Saturday night. Eat your cinnamon roll before it freezes."

"These are delicious. Don't tell my grandma, but they may be better than hers."

"Your grandma makes cinnamon rolls?"

"Only for Christmas. The best part of going to her house is her rolls. They almost make the hide-a-bed that was in use when Elvis was still alive worth it." Tessa studied the town square.

"Where does she live?"

"Near Manchester, Connecticut. As soon as I am finished, I'll drive up there."

They ate their rolls and listened to the music drifting up from the park. Tessa broke their silence. "Do you come up here often?"

"I used to every year with my dad to watch the tree lighting."

"You've mentioned your father a few times but always in the past. Is it too personal to ask?"

"My father was a New York City fireman. He was last seen running into the South Tower."

There were no words. Like everyone else, Tessa had watched the footage again each school year since that September morning in elementary school, but she'd never met anyone who lost someone. She found tears filling her eyes. She reached out for Sean's hand and held it. She didn't look behind her, where she knew she could make out some of the lights from the big city. There were enough pictures in her mind.

Neither moved during a rendition of "Good King Wenceslas" and "White Christmas."

"Thank you for not saying anything. Most people gush sentiments that are never very helpful."

"To be honest, I don't have words. Thank you for sharing."

Sean turned away from the belfry wall, and Tessa stepped into a hug without thinking. When the first note of "Jingle Bells" played, Sean gathered their garbage and opened the hatch. "Go first so I can lock this."

On their way down, Tessa paused at the door in the wall and waited for Sean. "What is in here?"

"The old balcony of the chapel."

All she needed was a rolled-up paper. Maybe it would be there.

A couple of vehicles blocked Tessa's car in the parsonage driveway.

"Well, I guess I am either waiting or walking." Tessa surveyed her car with her hands on her hips.

"I'll walk you to the inn." He offered his hand.

Tessa didn't take it. Instead, she pulled out her keys. "I think my tools may be safer in the catacombs." She hefted a large black bag from the trunk.

Sean took it from her. The bag was heavier than it appeared. "What do you carry in here? An anvil?"

Laughter answered him. "No, that would not be very useful. Just my soldering irons, a mini grinder, cutters, pliers, and other glass stuff."

She held the back door open for him.

"I am going to lock this stuff in Granda's office. Not that I am anxious about more things disappearing, but this is your personal equipment."

They double-checked the lock before leaving the church. This time when Sean extended his hand, Tessa took it. "Walk through the crowds," he pointed to the right and to the square, "or avoid them as much as possible?"

Tessa stepped to the left and the somewhat emptier street. Some people were starting to get in their cars, while others drifted in the direction of the train station. They passed several families and couples along their way. Sean looped his arm around Tessa's back and pulled her closer when they passed what looked to be some NYU frat boys who'd had one too many at O'Malley's.

"Hard to believe I was once that stupid."

Tessa shoved him with her shoulder. "You mean a drunk college kid or an NYU student?"

"I went to the University of Rochester, so just a stupid drunk college kid."

"Music major, then?"

Sean breathed easier when she didn't pursue the door he'd opened. "With a business minor."

Another group of college students passed them, running for the train station. Sean checked his watch. "They'd better hurry. If it is on time, they only have about two minutes."

"Do you always stay here? I thought your grandfather said you rented an apartment in the city?"

"I do, the same one I grew up in. I have been checking on Granda more frequently."

"You're afraid of losing him." No question mark punctuated Tessa's voice.

"Sometimes more than others. I think I would move away like Mom if it wasn't for Granda. There are organs needing tuning all over the country. And I don't relish the idea of living in the city my whole life. What about you? Where do you plan to go after you graduate?"

Tessa shrugged. "I don't know. I could go work in a studio or start one of my own. I like traveling and repairing glass, but as I learned in Europe last spring, hotels get boring after awhile. I'd rather have work come to me."

The train whistled. Three minutes late. Most likely deliberate to prevent stranded passengers. The street opened to the river. Lights of all colors bounced off its surface. Sean slowed his pace.

Tessa did too. "Will you be around tomorrow night or Saturday?"

"I should be here no later than seven tomorrow, and I'll stay all weekend."

"I'll need an extra pair of hands to extract the windowpane. Can you help me?"

"No problem." They stopped in front of the inn. Sean pulled Tessa in for a hug and dropped a kiss on top of her head.

She stepped back and looked up at him. For a moment he was tempted to kiss her as if mistletoe hung above them. Then the lobby door opened, and the moment fled.

"Sweet dreams, Tessa."

The walk back to the parsonage felt much colder.

thirteen

Reverend Cavanagh leaned heavily on his cane as he stopped to inspect Tessa's work. It seemed to Tessa that he was a bit pale. "Would you like my chair?"

"No, I've been sitting too much lately, I think. I haven't been getting my walks in like I should. Looks like you are doing good work. Will it be finished on time?"

Tessa swept up a bit of the copper foiling she'd trimmed away.

"Did you glue this?" He pointed to a place where there had been a hole earlier.

"No, I used an epoxy to fill in the spot where the pieces fit together with only the smallest of gaps, and since the hay was hand tinted, it seemed like the best option."

The reverend pointed to the area of most significant damage. "When are you starting on this section?"

"Sean is going to help me remove this pane in the morning. I need to work on it while it is lying down. See how the came is all twisted and torn? That is why I wanted the plans. I want to know precisely where the original lead lines were."

Using the cane to steady himself, Reverend Cavanagh stepped back. "I couldn't reach Nick, so I left a message on the answering machine over at the museum. I hope they get it. I liked it better when people answered the phones."

"Thanks for trying. Let me show you my drawings." Tessa spread out her sketches. "I made two variations of the section. There are not many photos of this part of the window, as people tend to focus on the center."

He picked up the papers and studied them closely. "I think this one is the closest. You would think of all people, I would know. I spent nearly every Sunday of my life either preaching in front of the window or staring at it while my father or grandfather preached. I honestly have no idea." He chuckled.

Tessa finished cleaning up. "I got a call from an antique store not far from here. They may have an old window with glass matching the broken piece in her dress."

"You'd buy used glass?"

"Old glass is even better than new glass sometimes as it has character the newer glass lacks. Considering my current choice is to replace this piece with something flat and almost the right color of blue, it is worth the drive to see what is in the window the shop found."

"Do try to get back early. Tonight is my favorite night of the festival—the judging of the Christmas cookies. I used to judge them every year. But my new doctor claims my body can't handle the sugar and put me on some pill. If it were really an issue, he would make me get shots."

"My grandmother is diabetic too. You should be thankful it can be controlled with a pill or two each day."

"Only one dessert a week. He is taking all the fun out of life." The cane thumped in emphasis.

"I plan on being back for the judging, and then maybe we can split a winning cookie." Tessa waved as she walked out of the back door.

Sean reached the parsonage as Tessa drove in. At least she'd come back earlier tonight. She got out of the car and kicked the tire before stomping into the church. Curiosity got the best of him, and he followed.

He could hear her voice as it echoed up the stairwell.

"How can someone get blue and orange mixed up?" Then, for a few moments, he only heard her footsteps. "But wait. It gets worse. He says 'I got another window, and it has blue and is all ripply.' Candace, it wasn't even real glass. It was some plastic aberration from the seventies. Remember the home-decorating book we mocked our sophomore year?" More footfalls. "Ten times worse. Then the guy tries to get me to go back to his storeroom. Coach Handsy with no charm. Where is Allie when you need her?"

Her voice grew softer. Sean knew he should make his presence known, but he continued to listen quietly. "So, I go outside, and Gertie refuses to start. I made a deal with her two weeks ago that if she got me through this job, I'd buy her a new battery. Mr. Antique offers to give the car a jump. Gertie starts, but the guy wants payment before he removes the cables!" Something thumped loudly. "That or pay him fifty, he said. So there goes all the money I earned this trip. The irony is I got paid to kiss a totally hot guy and spent it so I wouldn't have to touch a slimy fifty-something." The laughter he heard sounded like it had turned to tears. "Candace, I am a mess! Stop laughing!"

Sobs, not laughter reached Sean's ears. He wanted to run down the stairs but realized it might not be the best course of action.

"I've got to go. I promised the reverend I would go to the festival with him and try to keep him from overdoing it. He is type two, apparently, and is upset about not being able to judge the cookie contest."

Quiet shuffling. "Bye."

Sean retreated to the back door and opened, then shut it. Granda's voice echoed with "A lie is anything with the intent to deceive," but he felt less guilty than he should.

Tessa came running up the stairs and nearly barreled into him. He put out his arms and caught her. She folded into his chest and sobbed. Sean hugged her and wished he could do more.

After a few minutes, Tessa moved back and wiped her eyes. "Sorry for that."

"What's wrong?"

She wiped her eyes. "I went on a wild-goose chase, and my car broke down."

"Is that all?"

"Let's say I met a stereotypical macho guy who—" She bit her lip.

"Didn't treat you like the lady you deserve to be treated as?"

"That's one way of putting it." She managed a wan smile.

"Why don't you go in the ladies' room and wipe your eyes, and then we'll go get Granda. Cookie night is his favorite."

Tessa returned in a few moments. "Better?"

"You look better, but how do you feel?"

She straightened her shoulders. "I feel like going to find some cookies."

Sean smiled. "Let's go get Granda."

How was the cookie contest?

Candace's text had waited for almost an hour before Tessa was alone in her room and could answer.

— Fine. Sean, the reverend, and I stayed until the reverend got tired. Worried about him.

Need to talk?

— No. But, thanks. I'll call tomorrow, and we can chat. Is your dad there yet?

Sunday.

— Kk. Bye.

Tessa took a too-long shower trying to wash away the emotions of the day. Once again, she'd come up short on the glass. All her life she heard about Christmas miracles. Maybe this year she should do what all the glittery signs suggested and "Believe." But in what?

By the time she dried her hair and put on her snuggest sweats, she still didn't have an answer. She scrolled through her neglected emails. Araceli had written a long one, trying to convince her to do spring break in Haiti painting murals in an orphanage. While it sounded exciting, it wasn't appealing enough to try to scrounge up a couple thousand dollars to go. It was nice to see Araceli so excited as she struggled with the demanding art major.

Maybe Tessa had struggled once too and let her memory gloss over it. But it seemed from the first second she'd picked up one of the oil-filled cutters, Tessa knew glass was her specialty.

The email from her father started out with a photo of his current wife on crutches. Tessa didn't need to read far to know the plans for Park City were canceled. No, she didn't particularly want to go sit with them in their California condo. The last line caught her by surprise. Pregnant? Twenty-five years of being an only child and now she was getting a sibling who was due the week of graduation?

Most of the rest of the emails found their way to the trash bin.

Mandy's email brightened the inbox.

Okay, girls! Plans!

A car service will pick you up at Candace's on the 30th at noon. I am planning early because of weather. We are putting you up at the Four Seasons. Daniel insists he prefers it for security reasons, etc. I am not going to argue as they have an excellent spa. Here is a link to a formal rental company. Choose your three favorites and email me back. Do it soon while they still have

a selection. Daniel tells me I should have sent this link
before Thanksgiving. You can stay through the second,
right? Tessa, when do you need to be in Park City?

Hugs, Mandy

The dresses were gorgeous! Some of them almost made her want to dance the way they'd tried to teach her in the dance class she'd taken for a PE credit her sophomore year. But then she would need a plus-one.

Sean.

She hadn't even known him a week. A black-tie affair in another time zone wasn't exactly something one could ask someone to unless the relationship was definitely going somewhere. Nope, not the type of date you asked a guy on even if he did give you a perfect hug when you needed it and ended the night with a kiss on the cheek like he knew how vulnerable you still were after the events of the day.

She sent her reply to Mandy but only chose two dresses. Both blue. She would detail the Park City trip when they were together. If only Araceli could come too.

Turning out the light, she kept replaying the best part of her day. The hug.

fourteen

"ARE YOU FINISHED FOR THE night?" Sean's voice interrupted Tessa's thoughts.

"Just a little bit more." Tessa poised her glass cutter to make the first cut.

"You said that an hour ago."

Tessa looked at her phone—nearly eight. Where had the time gone? She planned on being further in her repairs before she quit. "I did, didn't I?"

"I saved some dinner for you. Come eat, and we can go watch the tree lighting with Granda."

Tessa set her protective glasses down and examined her work area. Because it was her habit to clean up after each step, she only needed to wipe her oil-filled cutter and put it away. "You're sure no one will come down here tomorrow?"

"I'll keep the key myself. The only reason to come down on a Sunday is to kick the old boiler anyway." Sean held up the key ring.

Looking over the room one more time, Tessa noticed the electric heater. "Oh, I need to unplug the portable radiator. Thank you. I can't believe how cold it got down here today." She also double-checked to make sure her equipment was unplugged and cooled.

"Ready?"

Tessa followed Sean out of the building. "When did it start snowing?"

"Must have been in the last few minutes." He held open the door to the house.

Reverend Cavanagh sat in his recliner. "About time you quit work for the day. Just because I am not paying you doesn't mean you can put in all the overtime you want."

Tessa returned his smile. "From the smell of dinner, I am getting paid pretty well."

"Well, I hope you can eat fast. The mayor will be upset if I am late tonight." He made an attempt to get out of the chair. Sean went to help him.

"Why will the mayor be upset, Granda?"

"Didn't I tell you? I get to flip the switch this year!"

Sean steadied his grandfather. "No, I believe you left that out of your news bulletins this week. Tessa, I am sorry to rush you, but—" He gave her an apologetic smile.

Using one of the soft rolls, Tessa made a fried-chicken sandwich. "Ready."

The doorbell rang.

"My ride." The reverend walked to the door, but Sean beat him.

"Come in, Ms. Mayor. Granda was telling me about getting to light the tree tonight."

"Isn't it exciting? Personally, I think the honor is long overdue. After all, your grandfather's little church is the heart of Christmas around here. Christmas won't be the same next—"

The reverend cut the mayor off. "No Christmas is ever the same, but we always have Christmas. Better get moving. I know you are worried about me being late, and we will be if you stand around yakking with Patricia."

Sean closed the door and shook his head. "Some days I think he takes his role as town grandfather too far. I doubt the mayor's own mother could be that brash and still loved."

"Face it. Your grandfather is one of those rare men who treats everyone like they are all his good friends, and everyone is." She went to the sink and rinsed her hands. "I am finished eating."

"Grab your coat and let's go. I want to see Granda's face when he flips the switch."

The snow still fell lightly. Sean liked this kind of snow—easy to shovel and not of epic proportions. A blizzard would ruin the evening. He reached for Tessa's hand, but she didn't take it. He found her catching snowflakes on her tongue with her eyes closed. He laughed.

Tessa closed her mouth. "I always like to try to catch one of the first snowflakes of the season, and we were running too fast earlier."

"I haven't tried since I was a boy." Sean joined her in catching snowflakes. Across the street, someone whistled. Sean reached for Tessa again. This time she took his hand.

They worked their way up near the front of the gazebo where city officials were already gathering.

"Sean, me lad, I see you still have the bonny lass with ye."

"I hear you haven't gotten your Irish and Scottish accents straightened out yet, O'Malley." Sean clapped his friend on the back.

"Why are you still with this boy-o? Most gals run from 'im after three days. Five be a new record."

Tessa didn't skip a beat. "And is your record still counted in hours?"

O'Malley laughed with them. "Sean, she is a keeper, and if you don't, I will."

Sean shot his friend a get-lost look.

"Lookee, there be a fine lass all alone. I must see if she needs me company."

The high school choir filed into the back of the gazebo, singing a song Sean didn't recognize.

The mayor accompanied Granda to the steps of the stand. "I could give a long-winded introduction, but everyone who has been in Blue Pines for more than a day knows Reverend Cavanagh and his catchall answer—"

"We have Christmas!" the crowd yelled.

The mayor laughed and turned to Granda, handing him the microphone. "We have Christmas—to remind us of all the things that matter. Family, love, kindness, and giving. We have Christmas so we can come together as friends, old and new, and so we can experience the miracles going unnoticed each day. But most of all we have Christmas to remind us to pause and remember God."

The crowd clapped. The mayor pasted on one of those smiles probably meaning "Have we offended someone?" For the first time in a long time, Sean found he didn't mind that Granda had managed to slip a tiny sermon into something. If he couldn't at Christmas, when could he?

The mayor took back the microphone. "Okay, time to turn around and watch the tree! You know what to do. Ten!"

"Nine, eight, seven, six, five, four, three, two, one!"

Sean watched Granda rather than the tree. He wished he could permanently capture the smile. From the flashes going off, there would be one in the morning newspaper or at least on a few social media pages. Granda gazed at the tree with all the wonder of a four-year-old. The cheers of the crowd decrescendoed, and the choir started singing a rendition of "O Christmas Tree."

Tessa retook Sean's hand and tugged him down. "Your grandfather is amazing." Tessa's eyes teared up.

He pulled her into a hug. "I know."

Standing among a throng of well-wishers, Granda was not leaving anytime soon. "Shall we go get some hot chocolate?"

"As long as we avoid the Homefire crew." Tessa nodded toward the tree.

"Belfry?"

Tessa nodded.

Coming up here was a mistake. There couldn't be a more romantic place in all of Blue Pines. Snow, Christmas music, hot chocolate, and even a hot guy who'd turned out to be much nicer than she expected.

Remember what O'Malley said—"Only five days"! Tessa was tempted to text an *S* to Candace. How long could she keep sipping her drink and avoid touching Sean again?

Sean rested his arms on the half wall. "I thought of watching the lighting with you from up here, like I used to with Dad. I've been thinking a lot about him these past few days, mostly because my mom is coming with her boyfriend and I think she wants to tell me she is getting married."

"Has she said anything?"

"Not specifically, but, well, something is different with her."

"How do you feel about it?"

"I love how Richard takes care of her, and he doesn't try to go all fatherly on me like some of her early boyfriends. Maybe it's my age, or maybe he realized Granda already took that role. He is good for her. And as Granda told me last September, we need to stop looking back."

Tessa moved next to Sean and put her arm around him in a half hug. She wondered how much of the concept of "stop looking back" applied to Sean.

"He has told me that every year, 'Stop looking back, or you will trip going forward.' I think I am starting to understand him now."

"What changed?"

She felt Sean shrug. "Maybe I am older, and a bit wiser. Maybe it's Christmas, like Granda says." Sean turned to face her, then lifted his hand to her cheek. It was still warm from holding his cup. "And may—"

Screams from the square caused them both to turn. What they saw caused her heart to skip a beat.

"Granda!" Sean flung open the trapdoor.

Tessa followed him. It took her a couple of tries to slide the bolt closed, and halfway down she realized they'd left their cups on the wall, but that could wait. Sean had already left the building by the time she got to the bottom of the stairs. At least she had her key and could lock the outside door.

Track had never been her thing, but her high school coach would have been impressed by how fast she ran around the church and into the square. The commotion was centered around the gazebo. The EMTs who had been on hand were rolling a gurney. She found Sean kneeling next to his grandfather and another EMT.

"Let me up. I only fainted."

"No way, Granda. Not until they check you out."

"Fuss and bother."

Another man pushed through the crowd. The EMTs let him pass. He conversed in low tones as the EMT took the reverend's vitals. "Well, Reverend, lighting the tree wasn't enough excitement for you? How about I recommend you leave this place under a set of flashing red lights? And I'll be right behind you."

"Aw, Doctor, it was only a little faint."

"For a man your age, there is no such thing." He nodded to the EMTs and left.

Sean stepped back and let them move his grandfather to the gurney. Tessa slipped her hand into his and squeezed. "What do you need me to do?"

Sean blinked a couple of times as if processing her words. "I left my car in the city. Will you drive me to the hospital?"

"Of course."

THE LIGHTS OF THE AMBULANCE flashed, the driver hitting the siren only briefly before pulling away from the curb. Sean watched, transfixed, until someone tugged on his arm and said something. Oh. Tessa. Granda would be dismayed to know his timing had interrupted Sean's attempt at romance.

Tessa tugged on his arm again. "Come on, Sean."

He followed her out of the square and around the church. A police car sat at the end of the driveway. The officer in it waved. "I came to give you an escort. Where's your car?"

Tessa held up her keys. "We are taking mine."

"Great! I don't need to worry about Sean's driving."

Sean didn't remember getting into the car or putting on his seat belt.

Tessa started the car twice. Sweet talk seemed to be her preferred method of car maintenance. "I'm glad your friend is giving us an escort. This traffic is worse than the other night."

Sean mumbled something. Mom. He should call Mom. He pulled out his phone. Voicemail. "Mom, they are taking Granda to the hospital. He argued with the EMTs, so I think he will be okay. I'll call when I know more. Love ya."

"Is there anyone else you need to contact?" Tessa kept her eyes on the road.

"No, my father, like me, was an only child of an only child, and I think everyone else in the town knows."

They pulled into the parking lot. Sean barely waited for Tessa to park.

"Go. I'll find you."

He sprinted across the lot.

The receptionist, a woman he knew but couldn't place, sent him back.

He turned around briefly. "There is a woman with blonde hair named Tessa. She'll be looking for us."

"Only family, Sean."

"Well, she is my, my—" He had no idea what to call her, but he knew the next little while would be more bearable for her if she could join him.

"Significant other?"

"Definitely significant."

"I'll try to sneak her back if I can." The lady winked.

Sean found the room and a feisty Granda.

"Tell them I don't need the IV, Sean."

Sean nodded at the nurse. "You know they wouldn't give you one if you didn't need it. Do I need to bribe you like you did me when I was five?"

"With a cookie?"

"Probably not with food. You will need to come up with something else."

"A kiss."

"You want me to kiss you, Granda?" Sean shifted to keep Granda's attention while the nurse drew blood through the IV tube she was inserting.

"No, kiss Tessa. You two are perfect for each other, but you only have a few more days. You got to let her know."

The nurse laughed quietly. "There you go. All done, Reverend."

"You tell him, Cheryl. Tell him Betty Everett was right."

The nurse shook her head. "I don't know her."

Granda looked the direction of the door. "Tessa, you know, don't you?"

"Know what?" Tessa slipped into the room.

"Betty Everett."

"Wasn't she a singer?"

Oh no. Sean knew with sudden clarity where Granda was going with this. Nana had played Betty's record over and over until it had worn out and Granda bought her a CD player.

"At least someone knows. Now, do you know what she sang?"

"Music?"

Sean breathed a sigh of relief when the doctor walked in, but it was short-lived.

"Doc, can you tell any of these kids what Betty Everett sang?"

"She sang several things, but she's most famous for the "Shoop Shoop Song." They probably know it as "It's in His Kiss." Now, why don't we clear this room and see what's going on."

The nurse had a hard time containing her laughter as she ushered them out. "I'll come get you from the lobby as soon as the doctor says you can come back. And thanks for distracting him from the IV and blood work." She turned down the hallway as Sean continued straight, her peals of laughter reaching his ears.

"Something tells me I don't exactly want to know what just happened." Had Tessa reclaimed his hand, or had he reached for hers?

"Granda was playing a game while the nurse got his IV in. He hates needles."

"Oh."

The lobby was full even for a Saturday night. It didn't take long to realize the majority of the people were here about Granda. Even Rabbi Goldstein had come.

Sean made the rounds with Tessa at his side, convincing most of them to leave. In the end, only Margo, Granda's housekeeper, and

Mr. Saunders, who played checkers with Granda every Thursday morning, refused to go home.

Sean and Tessa found a couple of uncomfortable seats in the corner.

"Do you want me to go find you some coffee?"

"No, I am fine so far, but thanks. I should try to call my mom again."

"I'll go talk to Margo." She gave his hand a squeeze before she left.

Sean dialed. "Hi, Mom."

sixteen

TESSA RUBBED HER EYES WHEN the glass in front of her started to blur. It had been a long weekend. She'd stayed with Sean at the hospital until they finally admitted his grandfather. After a twenty-four-hour observation, the reverend was released from the hospital late Sunday night. Taking insulin wouldn't come easily for the man. Sean had had to bribe him to even do a finger-prick blood test. Tessa did want to be there to see him make a snow angel or to hear Sean sing "O Holy Night," as she suspected he sang rather well with his knowledge of music. Each bribe was more creative than the last.

The two had argued enough over Betty Everett that Tessa spent a half hour surfing last night to learn about the singer. The "Shoop Shoop Song" replayed in her head. She turned on her Christmas playlist to drown it out. Picking up the cutter, she set the blade at the starting point.

The glass blurred again.

Maybe a quick walk would help her focus. Tessa made sure everything was unplugged and the light turned off before heading upstairs. Something banged on the front door, and then someone yelled.

Tessa went to open it.

"I was about to give up!" A man carrying two banker's boxes stepped into the building and walked to the last pew, where he deposited them. He then pulled a mailing tube out from under his arm. "I was told to find the things the reverend donated to the museum. Other than the clothing, this is it. Hope he finds what he needs." The man hurried back the way he came.

Tessa grabbed the tube and pulled off the end. A miracle! Annotated rubbings from the repair in the seventies. She rolled them up and put them back in the tube.

The only thing she immediately saw of note in the other boxes was an ancient leather-bound book. She flipped through it, noting it contained detailed notes from the builder. The drawing of a gargoyle stumped her. She hadn't seen any up on the roof.

She needed to share this with Sean and his grandfather. Besides, it was frigid inside the church today. Since the Sunday meeting had been canceled yesterday with Granda being out of commission, the heat hadn't been turned on entirely. She couldn't finish the windows wearing gloves. Maybe she could convince the reverend to let her turn it on for a few hours.

Grabbing the tube and the book, she headed for the parsonage.

Sean opened the door to a too-exuberant knock.

Tessa was practically bouncing. "Look what someone found!" She burst into the room like the sunshine he'd missed all day. "A man showed up with a couple of boxes and this tube. I wanted to get a better look at them, but the building was freezing. May I use the kitchen table?" She headed the direction of the kitchen. "How are you today, Reverend?"

"I'd be a lot better if that grandson of mine would stop hovering. Are those the plans you have been looking for?" He grabbed his cane and followed Tessa.

Sean shook his head. He hadn't been hovering. Trying to convince Granda he didn't need to dress in his "work" clothes and make calls had only partially worked as a stream of visitors came and went. Sean intercepted cookies and homemade candy all day. Why couldn't someone bring a nice baked chicken and lettuce or something? At least Tessa hadn't brought sweets with her.

She cleared off the table, then wiped it clean and dried it before opening the tube. "Look! Aren't these wonderful? I am so glad I got them. I completely missed this little sliver of lighter blue in my sketch. I'll need to trace it. If only I had my light table."

Granda spoke up. "I have a light table. It is only about a foot square."

"You do?" Sean and Tessa asked in unison.

"Yes, it was Cameron's. He used to draw. He made it one year. But he was never happy with it as the lightbulbs made it too hot. But those new curly bulbs they make nowadays might work better."

"Where is it?"

"Either in the sewing room or the cellar. Try the sewing room first. I think we kept most of his drawings up there, maybe under the bed."

Sean signaled Tessa to follow him upstairs. "Now you get to tour the home of a packrat. When you consider I am the sixth generation of Cavanaghs to live here, you can appreciate how deeply the tendency is embedded."

At the top of the stairs, he pointed out the bathroom and his bedroom. "That bedroom used to be Granda and Nana's, but she had problems with her hip the last few years, so we converted the small bedroom downstairs and the dining room to a master suite."

Sean opened the last door in the hallway. The room had once been decorated for a girl, in pinks and yellows. But the last time the Cavanagh clan had produced a daughter was three years before Granda was born. She'd died of the measles at age two.

"This looks a bit like an antique shop." Tessa turned around slowly.

"So, what would a light box look like?"

"I suspect it would be about this high." Tessa held her hands six inches apart. "And the top would be glass, possibly frosted." She knelt at the foot of the bed and pulled up the spread. Achoo!

"Dia linn."

"Dust bunnies."

"I would expect them to be bigger than bunnies by now," said Sean from the closet.

"I think I found something." Tessa pulled a portfolio and a box from under the bed. "Perfect. It is more like a foot and a half square." She peeked in the portfolio. "These must be your father's."

Sean sat down on the bed and looked over her shoulder. "I haven't seen these in years."

She moved each drawing carefully, as only an artist would, keeping her fingerprints off them. "Is this you?" A drawing of a little boy playing with a fire truck filled the page. "He must have loved you very much. The pencil strokes show so much feeling."

Sean swallowed. "I used to want to be a firefighter just like Dad."

Tessa tipped her head back, then set the portfolio aside and knelt, pulling him into a hug.

"I'd forgotten he even drew. Some days when I think of him, all I can see are those terrible replays over and over again."

"How do you know he was last seen going into the tower?"

"A woman he helped get out told us."

"Where is she now?"

"Someplace in the Midwest. She named her son Cameron." He buried his head in Tessa's shoulder and wept.

Tessa's knee started to ache, but she didn't dare move. Sean sat back and wiped his eyes. "I'll be back in a moment."

As soon as he left, she stood and rubbed her knees. Before closing the portfolio, she looked at a few more drawings. Sean should see the rest of these, but not today. The drawing of him wearing his father's turnout gear was precious. Tessa tied the portfolio together and left it on the bed. Before lifting the light box, she made sure to wrap the cord up so it would not trip her.

Sean met her halfway down the hall. She handed him the light box. "I left the portfolio on the bed. I think you should look at the rest when you are ready."

When they returned to the kitchen, the reverend was reading the builder's log book. "This is absolutely fascinating. And the drawings of the gargoyles—I have no idea what happened to them, but they were not there even when I was little."

"They are probably underneath the bed in the sewing room." Sean's words were meant for her ears only, but Tessa nearly ruined it by laughing out loud.

"Tessa, did you read this note with the rubbings?" Reverend Cavanagh pointed to a corner of the paper.

She read over his shoulder.

Packed remainder of glass with original glass in a wooden crate marked FRAGILE. Left in the cellar. PT.

"I didn't see any wooden crates. So close to another miracle."

Sean's head came up. "I know where it is!" He grabbed Tessa's hand, and they ran out of the house.

Tessa thought about her coat when the cold wind hit them, but she didn't care. Stopping only long enough to grab the Maglite out of the closet, they continued their wild run. Sean guided her through the maze of catacombs to the back corner. He swept the light across the room until it landed on the old crate. "I used to try to use this as a step stool to get out of the window."

Tessa inspected the box. "It looks like it is rotting. If it does have glass in it, I'd hate to lift it and have the bottom come off."

"Maybe we could roll it?"

If the glass wasn't packed well, rolling it could break some of it. "There is a metal 'Vote here' sign in room six. We could slide it under the crate and then move it."

They found the sign and with careful teamwork managed to move the crate to the work table. Using the screwdriver and hammer Tessa kept in her general tool kit, they pried off the lid.

"Oh! Oh! Oh!" Tessa grabbed Sean in a hug. "This is the best! Look! Not one but three sheets of the drapery glass. And all the rest!" She hugged Sean a second time and aimed a kiss for his cheek, but he turned his head and got it square on the mouth. A second of embarrassment flashed through her. *Oh no! What have I done?* But as Sean took control and deepened the kiss, the question fled like a ghost. A ghost she knew would come back to haunt her, but she wrapped her arms tighter around Sean and hoped the ghost had run far away.

seventeen

THE LATE-EVENING PHONE CALL INFORMING Sean the First Street Church's organ needed an emergency repair was a mixed blessing. It meant he would spend the next two days working and wasn't likely to get back to Blue Pines until late evening. It would be helpful for Granda to rely on someone else and to deal with giving himself the shots. The doctor had prescribed a special shot pen so Granda didn't need to see the needle, but it hadn't arrived yet. It would be harder to be away from Tessa for the day.

But then, being away from her for the day would give him time to clear his head. In less than a week, their relationship would be over. For the first time ever, he didn't want it to end.

Tessa ignored the early morning text from Candace. If she answered, she would have to tell her roommate about finding the glass, then the kiss, then the dinner with both Cavanaghs, then the walk home and the other kiss. Then Candace would YELL text or call—not a fun way to start the day.

Learning from the reverend that Sean had left early for the city hadn't been a good way either, but at least she could work without distractions. She carefully carried the drapery glass upstairs to the window and compared it until she found the right match. Working from the rubbing, she created the pattern for the new piece.

Cutting the glass proved tricky. Some old Styrofoam from one of the many boxes Reverend Cavanagh had collected proved to work well as a base after she carved out sections to support the drapery folds. She stopped to take photos to document the process. She doubted she would ever get to work with another piece of 125-year-old drapery glass again.

Then she began the painstaking process of replacing the broken piece in the still vertical window. At least Sean wasn't around to watch. She didn't need her hands shaking or her heart bouncing around in her rib cage as she manipulated the came or used the soldering iron. The fading light was not enough to get the full effect of the glass, but she didn't know where the switch to the floodlight was located.

Tessa smiled all the way back to the inn.

"Good day?" As usual, Margo manned the front desk.

"The best. I fixed the piece of the window I worried would be nearly impossible. I heard you teasing the reverend about saving everything. This time it was a blessing. Imagine holding a piece of glass that could have been ordered by Mr. Tiffany himself."

"You know, my grandma always claimed the window was one of his. But there doesn't seem to be much to prove it."

"There were many skilled artisans who worked with him, including several female designers. It is entirely possible the design came out of Tiffany studios, but not one of Louis Comfort Tiffany's works. Which, of course, is still amazing." Tessa let out a little sigh.

"Have you eaten dinner?"

Tessa shook her head.

"Well, head on into the dining room. Tell them to bill it to your room."

"But I am not paying for my room."

"Precisely." Margo waved her toward the door.

"I should change first? I am covered in dust and stuff."

"Don't dawdle. The chef's filet mignon is to die for."

And, as always, Margo was right.

Tessa stood back to admire her work. The redesigned section sparkled on the light table. As she worked the cement into the lead came, another worry plagued her—adequate time for the mixture to dry. At most, she only had about forty-eight hours before the section needed to be reinstalled. Ideally, she needed more than a week. She could only hope the recipe she'd learned from one of the studios she'd visited in London last spring would do the trick. It seemed to be working on the pieces she'd fixed in the vertical. At least with the exterior glazing she didn't need to worry overmuch about leaking. Still, she wished she had more time.

And not only for the windows.

The ghost that was born and fled with their kiss had seemed to multiply in the catacombs—a natural phenomenon in dark, musty places.

The boiler kicked on. The temperature must be dropping.

She brushed the excess cement away.

Familiar footfalls sounded on the stairs. "Still here?"

"As you can see."

Sean came around the table and studied the glass. "It looks done, but why are you spreading dirt on it?"

"It isn't dirt. It's cement. The cement seals and waterproofs it. Although there shouldn't be much water in here, I'm worried it won't dry in time."

"Would it help to move it up to Granda's office? The room is warmer as it is on a separate radiator link, or whatever you call it."

"Good idea. I'll take it up after I finish playing in the dirt and cleaning up."

"How long will that take?"

Tessa used her gloved finger to rub a section smooth. "Maybe an hour."

"I'll be practicing. Don't leave without waving goodbye."

"I won't." Tessa was by no means a music aficionado and had never spent much time listening to an organ outside of occasional church visits, but as she listened to the strains coming from above, she wondered if other instruments conveyed so much emotion.

After the last sounds of the *Messiah* faded, Sean played other pieces, some familiar, others not.

Tessa gave the glass one final rub. Now all she needed was time. She took the pane up to the office and found it open. Sean started a mash-up of carols. She went to watch.

His gaze met hers, but he continued playing until the end of the song. "Ready to leave?"

"Almost. I need to clean up and make sure the glass I purchased is packed well so I can return it tomorrow. I want to be here on Friday when the new exterior glazing arrives."

"You're driving to Jersey?"

Tessa nodded.

"Do you want some company? Unless I get another emergency job, I'm free, and it's good for Granda to rely on someone else."

"Sure, I'd love the company. My GPS is talkative, but he spends most of the time lying to me."

Sean laughed. "Would you like me to drive? I think my car is in a bit better shape."

"Sure. I better go finish up."

Sean launched into a tune she couldn't place, but it reminded her of background music to an old romantic movie.

eighteen

IF A CALL DID COME in asking for a last-minute organ repair, Sean was prepared to let his calls ring to voicemail. But his phone remained as silent as the early morning streets in Blue Pines.

Tessa waited at the hotel. She handed him a Styrofoam cup. "From Margo—the best raspberry hot chocolate I've ever tasted."

Sean preferred his unadulterated but took it anyway.

"I am assuming you know the basic direction. Believe me, we are better off not listening to my GPS app until we have to."

They swapped stories about favorite teachers and favorite roommates. Tessa mentioned that one of her roommates had married Daniel Crawford.

"You mean the rich-as-Midas guy always on the tabloid covers?"

"The very one. How often do you read tabloids?"

"Never. Haven't you ever walked down a street in the city past the newspaper vendors?"

Tessa pondered for a moment. "I guess I never noticed. I'm usually more focused on the museums I visit than the street vendors."

"Is that all you have done in the city, museums?" Sean switched lanes so he would be prepared for their exit. "No wonder you thought of the Met when I said Mets. I need to take you and show you the city."

"It would be fun, but I don't have time."

People rushed to finish their last-minute holiday plans, filling the freeway. He slowed to avoid someone who cut in front of him.

"This is worse than Chicago. Do you drive in this often?"

"I usually avoid the Jersey Turnpike, though I do get a few jobs in Newark and beyond." Sean switched lanes.

"I don't know that I could do this all the time."

"For the most part, I don't when I am working in the city. I plan my jobs so I am not trying to go from one borough to another on the same day. And often I'll take the train to Granda's. If I worked an office job, I wouldn't need a car."

"Seems odd to not need a car."

Sean laughed at Tessa's puzzled expression. "I remember one of the first movies I saw when I was maybe three. It was the first time I realized people lived in houses with garages and two cars. I mean, I knew Granda did. But I thought he was special. I thought most people lived in apartments."

"That would be weird, but I guess in most major cities, people do live in apartments or flats."

"I enjoyed living in the city, but I see why people want to move out and have more room. If it wasn't so expensive to move to one of the suburbs, I think I would." *Especially if I had a family.* The thought nearly choked Sean. Where had that come from? What about his vow to never fall in love and marry? Love hurt. Mom had been a mess for so long after 9/11.

"I think this is our exit. Do you want me to turn on the GPS so we can find the store?"

Sean was glad his thoughts were interrupted. "Why don't you. I don't think I have been here before."

The funny British voice got them to the glass warehouse, but Sean did wonder if it had guided them in a circle. "Remind me to look at your app. I think he is one tire short of a set."

Tessa laughed and opened her door. Sean noticed an auto-parts store next door. "While you return this, I am going to run next door."

Tessa picked up her crate of glass. "Would you mind getting the front door for me first?"

Nana would have banned him from her cookie jar for a week for his lack of manners. He should be carrying the crate, too. "Of course."

As soon as Tessa was inside, he hurried to the auto-parts store. It only took a minute to find what he needed. The clerk looked at him funny when Sean insisted he needed a bag but gave him one anyway. Sean beat Tessa back to the car. He wasn't sure how she would react to his impulse buy, but no way on earth would he let her leave Blue Pines without a new battery in that old car of hers.

The window company the reverend had hired knew their stuff. Tessa was relieved not to need to ask Sean to help place the window. How had she gotten herself into this mess again? She had to either part ways with Sean when things looked like they had a chance of being beautiful or try a long-distance relationship.

She decided to clean the window top to bottom on the inside as the workers from the window company wiped the exterior during the install process. And the new pieces were cleaner than the surrounding window. Standing on the ladder and using only water and her special cleaning cloths, Tessa reminded herself of all the reasons a long-distance relationship wouldn't work.

She'd proven the theory. After her weeks in Europe, she'd thought she and Gavin were something special. Upon her return to the States, they'd continued to exchange text messages and phone calls. Gavin had invited her to come visit him on multiple occasions. Driving back to college from a trip to Grandma's last August gave her the perfect opportunity to drop by.

She'd texted; he'd responded. She'd taken a detour.

The only person who seemed unsurprised when Gavin opened the door was Vanessa, her roommate for most of the Europe trip. In fact, clad in one of Gavin's trademark button-down shirts, Vanessa seemed downright pleased, her smile growing as the inevitable nasty insults, truths, and, finally, tears followed.

Tessa had cried through most of Pennsylvania and thought of nasty insults she would have liked to have said in Ohio. By the time she reached Candace's house in Indiana, she'd sworn off men and channeled her anger to turn the next four months' worth of Friday nights into a stained-glass window they installed in the library and two prairie-style windows for Mandy's new house.

Daniel liked them so much he offered her a business partnership if she ever wanted to open her own studio. She knew from watching *Shark Tank* that his terms were far too generous and turned him down. But he insisted the offer remained. Days like today tempted her to take him up on it. She loved glass, and having her own studio would be fantastic. If she started it near Grandma's, she would only be about two hours from Blue Pines. A two-hour drive wasn't exactly a long-distance relationship ...

She shook her head. What was she thinking? She'd never once considered setting up shop in Connecticut.

Standing on ground level, she finished the last pane and surveyed her work.

She heard someone come up behind her.

"You do great work. I've looked at that window for twenty-seven years, and if I didn't know where the repairs were made, I could never tell. Are you driving back to your grandmother's tonight?" Sean gave her a side hug.

Tessa shook her head. "I need to clean up my mess in the catacombs and all my tools. It will take me at least an hour to pack up, and then I need to pack at the hotel."

"Can you do clean up in the morning?"

The warmth spreading through her was all Sean's presence. "Why?"

"Because it's twenty minutes until the 5:15 train into the city leaves, and I think it would be a shame for you to be here at Christmastime and not see the Rock."

"The rock?"

"Rockefeller Center. You know, the place with the tree and ice skating featured in every Christmas movie ever filmed in New York."

"I'm a mess."

"If we hurry, we can stop by the inn and you can change."

"I'm in. Give me a minute to put this stuff away." Tessa waved to the ladder and her tools.

"I'll put the ladder away."

They took Gertie to the inn and then the station and had all of thirty-five seconds to spare. Sean gave Tessa the window seat. They were both breathing hard from the run across the lot.

"I can't believe Gertie started both times for us on the first try. It must be another one of your grandfather's Christmas miracles."

"It must be."

Tessa turned from the window and studied Sean, her eyes narrowing. "What did you do to my car?"

Caught. She was more perceptive than he thought. "Who says I did anything with your car?"

She poked him in the chest. "Me. Now spill."

"I may have given Gertie a new battery and cleaned a couple of connections."

"Sean, you can't spend that type of money on me."

"I didn't. I spent it on Gertie."

"How much do I owe you?" She poked him again.

Sean grabbed her hand. "Nothing. I used my movie money."

"I've priced batteries. Your movie money only covered half of it unless you found an amazing sale. Let me at least give you my movie money."

"But you already spent it." Too late, Sean realized his mistake. He saw the second Tessa knew it also.

"How do you know that?"

"I heard part of your conversation with Candace the other night. I didn't want to embarrass you, so I pretended I didn't hear you yelling."

Tessa sat back in her seat, but Sean didn't let go of her hand. They sat in silence while Tessa watched out the window.

He rubbed his thumb across her knuckles. "For about an hour I wanted to drive to every antique store I could find and punch every single guy I could find working at one."

The half-smile she gave him when she turned from the window made his heart do funny things it never did before, like grow three sizes and leave no room to breathe.

"I could be mad at you for listening, but you let me keep some shred of dignity the other night. And that is what I needed most. If I'd known you knew, I could have never gone and gotten cookies with you and your grandfather. Thanks." She leaned her head on his shoulder, and they rode in silence the rest of the way.

— **Rockefeller is so much better than in the movies!**

Candace's text came just seconds later. **Did you go alone or with Sean?**

— **Not answering. But the tree was amazing!**

Did you ice skate like they do in all the Homefire films?

— **No, but we ate chestnuts and window-shopped.** Tessa didn't tell about finding the perfect gifts for her roommates.

So, was it a date? Did he kiss you good night?

— **Maybe.**

So, you mean yes. You are so out of the club.

— I'll be leaving tomorrow.

Are you going to have regrets?

— Probably. I will always wonder what could have been.

Oh, girl. Hugs.

— Thx

What are you doing now?

— Cleaning up so I can go to Gran's in the morning.

Okay. Night.

— TTFN

Tessa started to sort the leftover pieces of glass. Some were too small to be useful, but it was a shame to toss the scraps. Tessa squinted and started arranging them. They began to take on a shape. It wouldn't take too long, and they would make the perfect Christmas gifts for the reverend and Sean. Well, she would add Sean's to the multi-tool she'd watched him play with in one of the stores. It wasn't the expensive one he examined longer, but he would know it was out of her college student budget.

She plugged in her soldering iron and went to work.

nineteen

AN INCH OF SNOW COVERED Gertie's windshield. It would be a white Christmas. Tessa hummed tunes as she loaded the trunk. Margo gave her some wrapping paper from the gift shop after Tessa told her about the stained-glass ornaments. She needed to wrap the ones for the Cavanaghs she'd left in the storage area and return the key.

Turning on Gertie's wipers, she couldn't help but wonder if the snow was beginning to fall harder now. She pulled in, turned the car off, and started toward the church.

What was that leaning against the back door? Halfway there she recognized the eight-foot-long boxes.

She turned and ran through the snow for the parsonage. "Sean! Sean!"

The door opened as she was lowering her fist to knock, and she hit Sean's chest. At least it hadn't been his grandfather. "The pipes! The pipes are at the church!" She grabbed his hand and pulled him after her. Sean quickly took the lead.

They ran up the stairs and stared at the boxes. "Where did they come from?"

Tessa searched for prints in the snow. "Where are your shoes?"

Sean looked at his bare feet. "Let's get these in the church, and then I'll go get some." He felt his pockets. "Do you have a key?"

Tessa produced the candy-cane-shaped ring and unlocked the door. They moved the boxes into the corridor.

"I can't believe it." Sean tried to pull the tape from the boxes. Tessa handed him the key to use. "They are all here, and they are repaired. How?"

Tessa ran her hand down the pipes, hoping to find a clue. "Look, a packing slip."

Only the address of the church and the list of repairs. Words in red ink replaced the spot where the dollar amount should have been.

Have a Merry Christmas concert. St. Nick.

"St. Nick?"

"Saint Nicholas, maybe?" asked Tessa.

"Granda is never going to believe this."

"Speaking of which, you need some shoes, and maybe you should dry your hair?" Tessa nearly added putting something on other than the thin T-shirt he wore, but she knew if she mentioned it, she would turn bright red.

Sean stood still, holding the key. "I am going to lock these in. I am afraid they are some sort of mirage."

"I think those happen in the desert, not in the snow."

They ran back to share the news.

The reappearance of the pipes perplexed Reverend Cavanagh too. "You are sure no one else was in the building that day?"

"I heard someone come in the back door. I assumed it was you. I didn't hear anything else for a minute or two. Then this man, Mick, or Rick, came looking for you. He didn't leave a message, but he did ask me about the pipes."

"How did he know about the pipes?" Sean practically yelled his question.

"I told him about them the night before at the inn."

A broad smile bloomed on the reverend's face. "I think I know who our pipe angel is. Nick."

Sean started laughing, then he grabbed Tessa in a hug and spun her around. "I don't know how you did it, but you managed to tell the one person in town who has the resources to help with the pipes."

"You know he will deny it," said the reverend. "So we are left with a Christmas miracle."

"Okay, Granda, I agree with you. We have Christmas!"

Tessa's phone rang. "Mom?"

The panic in her mother's voice echoed through the phone. "Are you driving?"

"No, I haven't left yet."

"Well, don't you dare in this snow. They're saying the nor'easter is turning into a blizzard!"

"A blizzard?"

"Yes, don't you dare drive, okay?"

"I won't."

"I'll call back later. Your grandmother wants me to check on her neighbor. Love you."

The television flared to life, the reverend working the remote. Every local station confirmed the news. All nonessential travel was discouraged as the storm had started.

The reverend lowered the volume. "Better bring in your bags. You can stay in the sewing room tonight."

"I'm sure I can go back to the inn."

"If as much snow falls as Channel 5 is predicting, we could well lose power. Margo will need those rooms for people with young children or stranded travelers. We own a real fireplace and lanterns. You'd better stay here."

Tessa looked at Sean. He nodded. "Why don't you get what you need out of the car, and I'll finish getting dressed. Then, if you would help me install those pipes—"

"Will there still be a Christmas Eve service?"

"Yes!" both Cavanaghs answered.

"We always have Christmas," added the reverend.

"The snow will stop in less than twenty-four hours, and almost everyone will be working today to keep the sidewalks clear. People will come out. We New Englanders don't let a few measly inches of snow bother us."

"The news said up to two feet. That isn't a 'few measly inches.'"

Both men laughed.

All things considered, it was a good evening. The pipes were installed, and his run through of various sections of the *Messiah* sounded so much better than the other evening. The power was still on, which, according to the news, put them in a better situation than many people. And he wasn't averse to having Tessa around for another day. During the installation, she had proven a valuable helper.

Right now she was challenging Granda in a game of chess and was a worthier opponent than most. Sean went to see if the sewing room was ready for their guest. On occasion, his mother stayed in the room, but the sheets could have turned to dust since the last time she visited.

His mother's flight had been delayed multiple times and finally canceled due to a storm in Florida.

He hesitated to think of his mom's delay as a positive thing, but he wasn't quite ready to introduce Tessa to his mother. He wanted to wait until … until what? He had no idea. He'd never wanted to introduce anyone to his mother before.

The portfolio lay where Tessa had left it. Sean moved it over by the door. The sheets both looked and smelled fresh. He pulled a set of towels out of the linen closet and added them to the bathroom.

The lights flickered. Sean found a flashlight, checked it for batteries, and put it on the bed in case Tessa needed it. Grabbing the portfolio, he headed downstairs.

Tessa was just putting up the chessboard, and Granda's seat was vacant. "He'll be back in a minute. I am going to make some hot chocolate. Do you want some?"

"Sure. I also thought we could finish looking at my father's drawings."

Tessa disappeared into the kitchen.

The tap-tap of Granda's cane echoed down the hallway. "I think I am going to tell you two good night. Chances are we won't be holding our morning service, but I want to make sure I am prepared, just in case. I don't know that I have ever gone two weeks in a row without preaching."

"Good night, Granda."

Tessa's voice echoed the sentiment from the kitchen.

Sean moved the couch closer to the fire.

Tessa brought in the hot chocolate. "I don't know if you like flavors in your chocolate, but I found these peppermint patties."

"I like mine pure, but I'll show you something with the patty." Sean unwrapped the candy and held it to his ear, where he broke it in half. "It sounds like opening a can of soda."

Setting her cup down, Tessa gave him a skeptical look but tried it. "Cool. Not quite ocean-in-a-seashell cool, but still pretty cool."

Sean drank most of his cocoa before opening the portfolio. "I would say I am surprised someone kept these all this time, but you saw this house and the catacombs, so you know I shouldn't be." He opened the portfolio, and Tessa scooted closer.

"Is this your mother?"

"I think that was about the time they got married."

The drawing of him in his father's turnout gear caught him off guard. Tessa leaned into him in a side hug. "How could I have forgotten? I would put them on and try to move. They were so heavy. Dad told me as soon as they fit, I could be a fireman

109

like him. Every birthday we would go down to the station and I would try them on. I assume he wore them that day. His body was among the 40% that weren't—" Sean felt tears gathering behind his eyes, so he leaned back and studied the ceiling. Tessa laid her head on his shoulder.

When Sean felt ready, he sat up and turned to the next drawing. Nana and Granda. "I think I should frame this one."

The last one was of him in his Mets cap at a game, sitting next to his father. He recognized it as his tenth birthday. The drawing wasn't finished, his father only lightly sketched in, unlike Sean's likeness. The photograph remained paper clipped to the corner, the paper clip having rusted and stained both the photo and paper.

"If you want, my old roommate Mandy is a master at photo manipulation. As in the CIA-wants-to-hire-her good. I am sure she could scan and repair the photo if you would like me to ask her."

"The negative might—"

This time the lights flickered and went out.

Sean closed the portfolio and set it on the coffee table. When he sat back, he draped his arm around Tessa's shoulder.

"At least we got to look at the whole thing."

"I'm glad you could be with me for this. I don't think I could have done it alone." Sean watched the fire. Yes, today had been pretty close to perfect.

twenty

TESSA WOKE UP SOMETIME DURING the night and found herself curled up on the couch, using Sean as a pillow. It took her a minute to realize the lights had come back on. Sean stretched and muttered something about Thomas Edison having impeccable timing before suggesting they go upstairs to bed. *Separately.* He repeated the word a couple times as he turned an awkward shade of red.

As predicted, the snow stopped by morning. By the time she got out of bed and was dressed, Sean had plowed most of the church's sidewalks. The reverend added his church to the list of those not holding morning services.

Wanting to feel useful, Tessa made biscuits and gravy and scrambled some eggs. She didn't quite prepare for Sean's post–snow blowing appetite, but no one complained. After breakfast, Tessa accompanied Sean back into the white world to look for neighbors needing help and to uncover fire hydrants. She now saw the wisdom in all the snow they'd removed during the storm yesterday. More than one elderly woman invited them in for a hot drink and some other treat. Every single one talked about how excited they were for that evening's concert and Christmas program.

Tessa found herself wondering if 7:00 p.m. would ever come.

Just as they were leaving the fourth house, her cell phone dinged. A text from her mother.

Power is out. We are at Grandma's church as they have a generator. Please don't come yet.

Tessa pictured the modern building her grandmother attended each Sunday.

— Are you safe and warm?

Yes, but I know they have the freeway open. I don't want you to come yet.

— I was going to wait for tomorrow. The news said they were asking people to limit nonessential travel.

I knew I raised a smart daughter!

— Love you

At five o'clock she accompanied Sean to the church to "check on things," as he told his grandfather. They were met by choir members from the various churches who had come to do a quick run-through of key parts of the night's performance since they had been unable to practice in the church and keep the surprise. Several of the choir members were missing for various reasons, mostly power-outage related, but a few people had chosen to leave town to visit relatives ahead of the storm.

After the practice, Sean and the choir director discussed their disappointment as the effect was not as strong as they hoped.

Tessa bit her lip. She had an idea, but would they like it? "What if you turn the program into a sing-along?"

Both men turned toward her. Sean answered, "A what?"

"When I was twelve, I went with my grandmother to a sing-along *Messiah*. During the chorus, the director would turn to the audience and have them join in."

The director rubbed his chin. "That would work, but where would we get enough copies of the music on time?"

Sean scrolled through his phone. "It's on the internet. People with smartphones can look the music up."

Tessa couldn't hide the excitement in her voice. "There are more than a hundred copies in the second storeroom in the cata—I mean cellar."

The choir director smiled. Sean looked surprised. Both men followed Tessa down the stairs, where she quickly located the box of sheet music. The director flipped through a copy. "These are perfect. A sing-along it is!"

Another surprise awaited Sean as he and Tessa returned to Granda's to change. A car with Florida plates sat in the driveway. Sean opened the door to the house and blinked twice. Mom and Richard sat on the couch. They both stood as Sean approached.

"Mom, what are you doing here?"

"You think I would miss tonight's service?" Mom pulled Sean into a hug.

Richard extended his hand. "I'd say she made me drive, but I wanted to come as badly as she did. The drive didn't get bad until into New Jersey. I'd say New York is at the southern end of the storm. By the time we reached here, they'd opened enough major roads that with the help of our GPS, we found our way."

Sean turned to Tessa. "I think you need to get whatever app my mom—Roberta—and her—"

"Husband."

Sean's head whipped back around at his mother's announcement. His mom held up a hand, showing a beautiful diamond-and-ruby wedding set. "We got married on the cruise this summer. I wanted to tell you in person."

"Wow." Sean gave his mother and Richard a hug. He fluctuated between disbelief and the feeling it was about time. "Congratulations. I admit I wish I had been invited. But I am very happy for you."

"It was kind of a last-minute thing. We were with Richard's daughter getting her license, and the next thing we knew, we were getting one too."

"Not like I hadn't proposed to your mother a half dozen times over the last couple years." Richard put his arm around Sean's mom.

"You even asked my permission. I thought you'd chickened out." Sean laughed.

Mom turned to Tessa. "Now, I believe you were about to introduce us."

"This is Tessa. She repaired the Nativity window."

Tessa shook both Richard's and Mom's hands.

"Granda was telling us about you. He is so pleased with your work."

From the smile on his mom's face, Sean had the distinct feeling Granda had told her much more. The hall clock chimed the half hour. "We really need to get ready. Where are you staying?"

Granda spoke up. "I put them in my old room since Tessa is in the sewing room. But you are right. We'd better hurry!"

The final notes of the *Messiah* faded away. From the smiling faces around her, it was evident Sean had more than accomplished his goal. Tessa smiled up at Sean. He was grinning ear to ear. No doubt the trumpet pipes had added to his smile. She couldn't wait to talk to him.

Reverend Cavanagh stood. "Thank you for coming to the annual concert. It is tradition that we go out singing carols to those who could not join us tonight. For those of you who can join us, we'll make our usual four groups. Those going north on Main, meet in the back left corner." He pointed. "South on Main in the right.

East on High Street up here, and West over there. As soon as you are assembled, my grandson will start us off with "Silent Night." Remember to start singing as you file out."

An organized chaos followed. Tessa joined Roberta and Richard near the pulpit, Sean played an introduction, and everyone started singing. The groups each left as they had for generations.

As they filed out, Sean finished playing the first verse and let the music fade. Then he turned off the organ and came down to join them.

His grandfather hugged him. Tears were in the older Cavanagh's eyes. "Why didn't you tell me you were bringing back the *Messiah*?"

Roberta explained to Tessa, "About five years ago we couldn't get enough choir members to join us, so we canceled the *Messiah* portion. Margo always manages to find enough children to be in the pageant and puts any extra children who come in angel costumes and shepherd robes. Since I read the Christmas story from the Bible, they don't need more than one practice. Then we would carol."

Sean and his grandfather broke apart. Tessa could see tears in Sean's eyes as well. "I'd better go ring the bell. Do you want to come, Tessa? I brought an extra set of earplugs."

Roberta gave Tessa a nudge. "I'll go get the wassail ready."

Once again, Tessa followed Sean up the winding staircase. Halfway up, Sean unwound a rope from a hook on the wall.

"That rope wasn't there last time, was it?"

"No, I came and connected the bell on Friday. Even a few inches of snow make opening the trapdoor difficult. Besides, we don't want to be up there when it rings." He let the rope uncoil to floor level and motioned for Tessa to go back down.

When they reached the bottom, Sean checked his watch. "Only two minutes."

"You ring the bell at ten?"

"Yes, all the other churches ring their bells at midnight. But they turn their bells off for the 10:00 p.m. chime on Christmas eve so the old church can be the first to ring in Christmas."

"That's a fun tradition."

"Put in your earplugs and cover your ears."

Sean pulled the rope.

Dong. Dong. Dong. Dong. He smiled at Tessa as he finished the tenth pull.

Christmas was officially here.

twenty-one

SEAN TUGGED TESSA'S HANDS FROM her ears and pulled out his own earplugs. She did the same. He wanted to pull her into a hug and kiss her soundly, but she exited the stairwell before he had a chance.

The exterior floodlight illuminated the Nativity window. As Sean and Tessa stopped to look at it, he put his arm around her. "You did an excellent job. Tonight wouldn't have been right without it."

"I think your music made tonight really special. I am so glad those pipes showed up."

Sean started to turn for a kiss, but Tessa stepped away.

"I'm looking forward to your mother's wassail." She hurried across the sanctuary to the back door. He followed, wondering what was wrong.

Christmas tunes played from the old stereo. Mom stood in the kitchen, stirring a pot. Granda sat in his chair while Richard fixed the fire. Tessa went to help his mother, or to avoid being with him. He wasn't sure, so he joined the men.

Richard sat on the couch next to him and nodded to the kitchen. "Do you think she will be with us next year, too?"

Sean blinked at the question. He had never had a relationship last more than a few weeks. Richard knew that.

Granda spoke up. "It would be nice if she was."

The women laughed in the kitchen. Sean looked over, hoping they hadn't heard. They came out carrying one tray laden with cups and another filled with goodies. Tessa sat in the other chair, and Mom joined Sean and Richard on the couch.

Granda picked up his cup. "Am I allowed to drink this?"

"I made yours special, so there is no extra sugar. But we will check your blood before you go to bed." Mom's years of nursing gave her the knowledge to deal with Granda.

Tessa's phone rang. She excused herself to the kitchen.

She came back smiling. "My mom and grandma are back in Gran's house."

Tessa didn't say what Sean already knew. She'd be leaving first thing in the morning.

The family continued to eat and talk until Granda fell asleep in his chair and Mom woke him. "I guess it's time for us to go to bed."

Granda yawned. "Good thing I don't do a midnight service. Sean, will you go ring the bells at midnight?"

"You know I will. I can't let the others ring without us. Night, Granda."

Tessa started to clean up. Sean went into the kitchen to help, and she handed him a drying towel.

"So, you are leaving in the morning?"

"Yes, thank you for letting me stay. Tonight was incredible."

"But you'll be back."

"Maybe someday. Everyone comes to New York eventually. But I don't really plan to."

"Don't you need to check on the window?"

Tessa studied the soap suds. He couldn't see her face. "I should, as I am worried about the cementing, but, Sean, I can't come back."

"Why not?"

"Because I can't do it again." She kept her back to him.

"Do what?"

Tessa didn't speak for a couple minutes, but when she did, she didn't look at him. "I'm sorry, Sean. I shouldn't have kissed you or let this become more than casual. I mean, this is more, isn't it?" She didn't wait for an answer. "I can't do another long-distance relationship." Tears trailed down her cheeks.

"Who broke your heart?"

She shook her head. "Does it matter? I wish ..." Tessa blinked up at him, then ran up the stairs.

Sean rang the midnight bell alone. He sat in the church, staring at the window for what seemed like an eternity before shutting off the outside light and locking up.

The alarm went off at five. Tessa silenced her phone before the second beep, then quickly got dressed and made the bed.

She negotiated the staircase without turning on the light or dropping the suitcase. Light from the dying fire guided her as she set her two packages under the tree and contemplated where to leave the note for Sean.

"Are you really going to leave without saying goodbye?"

Tessa jumped at the sound of Sean's voice.

"Did you sleep there?"

Sean stood up from the couch. "I was waiting for Santa."

"Oh."

"No, Tessa. I couldn't let you go without saying goodbye." He opened his arms for a hug.

Tessa hesitated only a second before stepping into his arms. She didn't want to leave. For a minute, she didn't care what she'd written in the note. Maybe they could work something out.

When Sean kissed the top of her head, she turned her face up to meet his, and their lips met. The tears she tasted had to be more than her own. She ended the kiss, set the note on the table, and picked up her suitcase.

"Here. Don't forget your gift." He handed her a wrapped box about the size of a book.

At the door, she waved. If she opened her mouth, she would start crying harder.

twenty-two

GERTIE ROARED TO LIFE, AND she was gone. Maybe he shouldn't have purchased the battery after all.

He picked up the letter she'd left on the table. He didn't want to read it. She had been going to tell him goodbye in a note. He had been right to vow never to fall in love. For a few crazy minutes, he'd thought long-term, as in the big M word.

The fire crackled and popped. Sean added another log to it and turned back to the couch to find his mother there.

"She is different, isn't she."

For a moment, he thought of denying it, but lying to one's mother was never a good idea. "She was only here two weeks, but, yes, she is different, probably because she isn't the type of girl I normally find."

"You mean she wasn't looking for a temporary man?"

"I don't think she was looking at all. If it hadn't been for the movie director, I don't even know we would have gotten past friendship."

"Movie director? Maybe you should tell me more."

Sean found himself telling his mother things he'd never dreamed of sharing with her. Somehow he even told her about the vow he made after Dad had died.

"That explains a lot. Yes, I was a mess after 9/11, but it wasn't just losing your dad. I was assigned to orthopedics that day, but since I have experience as a triage nurse, I was called down to the ER. I still ..." Mom grew silent. "Thinking about 9/11 is hard. I knew the wives of so many other firefighters. We always knew the possibility existed of them not coming home from work one day. But we never imagined ..." She paused again and blew her nose. "Richard has been so good for me. For a while, I think I dated any man who came along. I tried to keep them a secret from you, but I think you knew."

Sean nodded.

"Anyway, once you went off to college, I realized I needed to change things. Cameron would not want me to live like I was dead. I love working at the retirement center in Florida. Most of the residents are active and don't need me much. Many are widows who talk of their husbands and the fond memories they shared. Others are bitter about their lives and not very fun to be around. I didn't want to be one of the latter. Richard showed me how to have fun again. He waited while I healed. He even asked me to go see a counselor."

"Like we did after?"

"Not exactly. This wasn't all about dealing with grief. This was about dealing with life. September is always going to be hard for me. But it is easier with Richard. I let those terrorists take more than my husband from me. It took me years to take my life back. I don't want you to lose your life over that day too."

"We found Dad's drawings. I forgot so many fun things about him. Looking at them with Tessa, well, it was like it was okay for me to feel again. She didn't say any of the stupid things people usually say." Sean leaned back on the couch. "I think I want to frame a couple of them. But what I really want—" Sean left the sentence hanging. What he wanted was to see if Tessa matched him as well as he thought she did.

"Then find a way to go after her."

Sean shifted to stand. "How? I don't even know where she went."

Mom pulled him into a hug. "You'll find her. After all, how many Tessas in the world do stained-glass?"

My email is glassgirl@college …

Even with Grandma's cinnamon rolls, Christmas had lost some of its luster. Tessa knew it was because she'd left part of her heart in Blue Pines. She rolled over, searching for a comfortable spot on the hide-a-bed. Had she done the wrong thing? An image of Gavin answering his door popped into her mind, his face fading into Sean's. Drat her artistic imagination.

An alert chimed on her phone. Maybe it was Candace. She hadn't dared bug her on Christmas.

An email from Sean@organrepair.com

She bit her lip and opened it.

> Tessa,
>
> Thank you for the bell ornament. Granda loves his star and cross. I know you deliberately didn't give me your contact information, but when we met, you told me your email. So I did come by this legitimately.
>
> I don't agree with your note, but I understand you have been hurt. Will you give me a chance to at least write you for a while?
>
> Please let me know you made it safely. There have been more accidents than usual today.
>
> Always, Sean

Tessa reread the note. It would be rude to not respond and let him know she arrived safely.

Sean,

The drive took a little longer than I planned. I am glad I used the app Richard suggested. Thank you for the scarf and hat. I forgot I gave you my email. You can write, but I don't know if I will respond. Please understand.

She rewrote the line three different ways and then left it. He had her note that explained in vague terms about being hurt, and he said he understood.

Have a happy New Year!

Tessa

Sleep didn't come any easier after she hit Send.

In a couple of days she would be in Chicago. Mandy might have some good advice. After all, she and Daniel had worked the distance thing. Only their relationship was different. Daniel had fake-dated half the actresses in the country openly but never took them home.

Maybe love wasn't supposed to make sense.

twenty-three

THE ORGAN SOUNDED HER BEST the morning after Christmas. Sean played a few of his favorite toccatas and a fugue. Granda's cane tapped against the floor. Sean took the sound as a message to stop.

"Come talk with me."

Shutting down the organ, he joined Granda on the front pew. "Nick Gooding will be here in a moment. I've wanted to talk to you, but with Tessa here, I never found the right moment. He has a bunch of paperwork for me. I want to give you my $2,000 rainy-day fund. The board also decided to sell the church to the Goodings to be part of the museum complex."

"What?"

Granda held up a hand. "You know as well as I do my congregation has dwindled to nothing. Neither you nor your father had any inclination to the family business. Nick wants to turn this into a concert hall and community center, which is all it is anyway. He is going to sell me back the house for $100, the same price the Cavanagh's sold the house to the church for all those years ago, and I want to give it to you. That way when Nick hires you as the caretaker, you'll have a place to live, and you don't need to give up your business in the city."

"Granda, I don't even know what to say. Did Nick say he would hire me?"

"Not in so many words, but you know he will. You don't need to take the offer if you don't want to, but I know how you love this building even if you are not disposed toward religion. I've watched you over the last few years with your love/hate relationship with New York. I think if you could finally give up the apartment, you might like it here."

"I would. I could teach here, couldn't I?"

"I am sure Nick wouldn't have a problem with it."

"What are you going to do?"

"I've been talking to Roberta about that senior-living place of hers. With my diabetes getting worse and New York getting colder ..." Granda shook his finger. "Don't you say anything about global warming. I say it is colder. Anyway, it makes sense. Your mom and Richard have also asked me to tour Ireland with them in the late spring. Won't that be grand?"

"I'm not sure what to say."

"Take some time to think about it. I don't think Nick needs an answer today. He said he needed to have a long talk with you."

As if on cue, Nick and his lawyer came through the back door.

Sean sat across from Nick Gooding and his father, Ansley, with one of Granda's banker's boxes at his feet. "So what you are tell-ing me is that Granda's $2,000 rainy-day fund that I have heard him talk about his entire life is worth 1.8 million."

Ansley leaned forward. "No. 1.8 billion, with a "B". But after the taxes are settled it will be closer to 1.2."

Sean shook his head. "I don't understand. How could Granda's $2,000 become so much without him knowing?"

Ansley pulled out a legal pad. "Well, it all started in 1957. When Reverend Cavanagh was twenty, his maternal grandfather died leaving him $2,000. My father talked him into investing it in a little company called American Centry Investment Firm. Unbeknownst to you, your grandfather, his father, Cameron, added another thousand to the investment bringing the total to $3,000. Then your great-grandfather told Reverend Cavanagh to save it. Following me so far?"

"Yes, I have known all my life about the fund. Being born near the end of the Great Depression, Granda always saved everything. Even if he didn't read it." Sean nudged the box at his feet filled with unopened statements dating back more than four decades.

"To make a long story short, the investment remained untouched. It multiplied and spilt. I recall my father trying to convince the reverend to do something with it, but he wouldn't touch it. Your grandfather is as stubborn Irish as they come and refused to believe it could be worth more than his original $2,000. He did give our investment firm some power over it, so any taxes due have been paid as the dividends were reinvested." Ansley wrote on the notepad.

"This is where I come in. As you can imagine the Cavanagh fortune has been something of a running joke in our family my entire life. But because of privacy we could never say anything to you. Earlier this year the Reverend asked me if it was better to give you his rainy day fund now or leave it to you in his will. He had read about inheritance taxes and was afraid you would only get a thousand dollars."

Both Nick and his father stifled laughs.

"Anyway, you know how your grandfather is about making a decision. He kept putting it off even after I explained that taking care of things while he was living was the best course to take. He called me the morning he got home from the hospital and asked me to transfer the fund. He said he thought you would need it to buy a ring soon."

Sean felt his face heat.

Ansley laughed. "I keep hoping Nick will need to do the same thing. We rushed the paperwork to have the transfer under this year's tax laws. It isn't a transfer as much as you are now a joint account holder with your grandfather."

"Oh, that makes it better. I only own half of 1.8 billion. I can't even start to comprehend this. No wonder Granda didn't want to hear about it."

Ansley turned the pad to Sean. "I think you are going to owe roughly 600 million in taxes since this is triggering a tax event, but that is something for our CPAs to figure out."

"Just think, your taxes can single-handedly fund a government agency for a year."

Sean gave Nick a wry smile. "Just what I have always wanted to do. I don't even know how to handle a million dollars. What am I going to do?"

"Don't worry Sean. We will be here for you as friends and as your investment firm. The next few months will probably be the hardest. Eventually the media will get wind of this, and every long-lost aunt and her twenty cats is going to be asking you for a donation or a loan. You probably will want to find a charity, but ignore most of the requests." Ansley's reassurance didn't help much.

"I'll be honest. The worst thing about having money is the dating. I never know what impresses her most, my witty sense of humor or my ranking in the three comma club." Nick shook his head.

How would Tessa take the news? Having money could change the way their long-distance relationship worked. What if he partnered in her glass studio? How do you even tell someone that you just inherited an insane amount of money? Other questions raced through Sean's mind at a dizzying pace.

"Breathe Sean. You look like you are thinking yourself right out of the room." Ansley handed Sean a water bottle.

"It is going to still be a few days before you have full access to your funds, and even then it isn't like you can go buy a Manhattan high-rise. However, we thought you might like to be part of the Blue Pines Museum project."

Sean thought he knew where Nick was headed. "So I buy the church?"

Nick nodded. "The papers we gave your Grandfather and the church board are a bit vague on who the buyer is since the Blue Pines Museum is an educational non-profit. Basically, you sign these forms donating the funds to the Museum project and this one accepting a place on the board, and you buy the church for the community."

"Where do I sign?"

Nick stuck out his hand. "Welcome partner."

Tessa,

It has been a couple of very odd days here. There is so much I want to say but I don't even know where to start. Would you give me your phone number please?"

Hope you are having the best of days,

Sean

Her fingers hovered over the keyboard for a moment before she responded.

Sean-

Is your grandfather alright?

T.

The reply came back in minutes.

Granda is the same. Making plans to move to Florida.
He sold the church to the Blue Pines Museum and
gave me the house.

Phone number please? Mine is 212-555-5683.

Sean

Tessa picked up her phone and prayed someone would answer.
"Hello?"
"Candace? Help."

Two days later, Sean walked into Nick's New York office. The
secretary told him to have a seat in the waiting area. since he
didn't have an appointment.

"Sean, you have perfect timing. I have a clear calendar for at
least an hour. Coffee?"

Sean shook his head, and Nick dismissed his secretary.

"I keep thinking this is some huge joke. I don't even know
where to start."

"Keep it simple for now. Don't go buying anything huge. Use
the money to help your Granda with his retirement."

"He spent a half hour last night preaching on the ninth com-
mandment. He thinks I am lying about the money."

Nick laughed so hard he had to turn to the window to compose
himself. "Now you know what we have been facing all these years."

"For years I dreamed of buying Granda's house, someday and
somehow, and live there. I guess it is mine now anyway, but can
I live there?"

"Why not? Put in an alarm system. Your neighbors aren't going
to bother you much. We have an extra office here. For now you
can use it so you can list it as your business address instead of
the apartment. Once Forbes figures out that you belong on their
annual list, you'll want a personal assistant anyway."

Personal assistant? Forbes? Sean shook his head. "You mean I would need to work here? I'm still trying to figure out what to do about repairing organs."

"No, you can do whatever you want to. It is just a space you can rent in the interim. Repair organs. Work on the Blue Pines Museum. Hide out from life."

"How involved can I be with the Museum project when it comes to the church?"

"As hands on as you want to be. It might help you to focus on that for a while anyway. Deal with fixing the old building as well as play several concerts during the year and on Christmas Eve. I also hope you will work with the Museum. There is enough history hiding in the cellar of the old church to fill half of it."

"I think I can do that."

"It is completely selfish, I assure you. It wouldn't be Christmas without the church, and besides, someday our children will need to play hide-and-seek in the basement." Nick smiled.

"We need to be clear that the boiler room is off-limits."

Nick pointed at Sean. "As I remember, you hid in there."

Sean pointed back at his childhood friend. "But you are the one who locked the door. Granda was frantic when he finally found me. I banged on those old pipes so long he thought the place was going to blow."

"Maybe we won't let our children play down there. Not that I should worry. I still need to find a wife."

"Me too."

"What about the glass girl I saw you with? It looked like you two had something going on."

"She left. Doesn't do long distance. We were emailing, but she didn't return my last one."

Nick leaned forward in his chair. "Oh? Anything I can do to help?"

"Short of getting me into Daniel Crawford's New Year's bash? Probably nothing," Sean joked.

"Why there?"

"Tessa was roommates with Mandy Crawford, and it's the one place I know where to find her without becoming some creepy stalker."

Nick moved some papers around on his desk, then punched his intercom. "Do you know where the invitation to Daniel Crawford's New Year's Party in Chicago went?"

"Yes, it's in my decline-and-thank-you box."

"Can you bring it here?"

The secretary opened the door and handed Nick a paper. Nick read it and gave it to Sean. "I'll drop Daniel a text to let him know you are crashing."

"Really? Just like that? I'm going?" Sean sat dumbfounded not sure if this was due to friendship or his new financial status.

Nick leaned back in his chair. "I saw you together. If I had a girl who looked at me like that, I'd go farther than Chicago to get her back."

"I don't know what to say."

"How about thanks, and then hurry on out of here and make sure your tux is clean?"

"Tux? I guess I should go buy one."

Nick typed into his phone. "I just texted you my favorite shops. Tell them I sent you."

Nick walked Sean to the door. "Do you want my secretary to book a flight?"

"No, I think I'll drive."

"Good luck!"

twenty-four

SHE DIDN'T BELONG HERE. THE rented dress, the too-tight shoes, the hose—whoever invented these torture devices must have been male and semi-sadistic. She wondered if anyone would notice if she slipped into the ladies' room and donated them to the rubbish bin. Would anyone notice if she slipped out? Would anyone notice if she stood on her head?

Not likely. Standing between a potted tree with twinkly lights and a painting of tulips—probably an original Georgia O'Keeffe—Tessa felt every inch the wallflower. Even the toenail peeking out of the open toe of her shoe had a flower on it. This morning during her pedicure with Candace and Mandy, she'd pretty much told them everything. To her surprise, both girls urged her to get back to New York as soon as possible. Candace had twirled the curls in her new auburn wig. "Girl, Sean is nothing like Gavin. Remember all the pressure he put on you? Sean didn't do any of that." Mandy pointed out that Tessa really didn't need to be at the school more than a couple weeks all semester and Daniel's business loan offer was still on the table. They'd even lined up the first commission for her—ironically, a flower-motif window for the old Crawford Mansion community center.

The newlywed Crawfords were speaking with several people she didn't know near the door. Mandy's hand rested on her—No way! Could Mandy be expecting? Tessa searched for Candace. Surely she would know. Candace's soft champagne curls were easy to spot on the dance floor. Wow! Who knew Mr. Computer could dance the waltz like Fred Astaire? They looked like one of those couples on a reality dance-off show. As far as she knew, Candace hadn't taken dance since she was fifteen, and that had been ballet. Tessa wished Araceli had come. Then she would have someone to gossip with. Even Bonnie and Mr. Morgan were dancing.

Tessa watched as Colin and Candace danced to a new song. A rumba? A tango? Honestly, she had no clue. She absently toyed with the little beaded bag Mandy had given her to match the dress. She could feel the hotel key card sliding around next to her phone. Really, no one would notice if she slipped out. Once she found a cab, she would text Candace so she wouldn't worry. The last thing she needed was Alex and Abbie, Daniel's ever-present but discreet bodyguards , searching Chicago for her.

She turned to go and bumped into a man who reached out to steady her.

"Oh, pardon me," she said, addressing his shiny shoes, too embarrassed to see which of Chicago's jet set she'd bumped into. Bad manners, but if it was one of Daniel's famous friends, she would either faint or cry, and that would be worse.

The hand did not let go when she tried to step around him.

"Tessa." No mistaking the New York accent, but here?

Tessa blinked twice. She laid her free hand on his chest and was reasonably confident she couldn't hallucinate a heartbeat. But she hadn't touched a drop of alcohol all night. "How? Why?"

Without a word, Sean lowered his head and kissed her like the entire ceiling was coated in mistletoe. Betty Everett had won. The answer *was* in his kiss.

"I know that doesn't explain everything," Sean rested his forehead against hers, "but I hope it helps cover the why. Tessa, you make my world sparkle, and I don't want to lose you or us. I know these next few months will mean a lot of traveling back and forth, but we need to try."

"You are willing to come out here for me?"

"Perhaps I didn't do it right the first time." Sean pulled her close for another kiss.

Tessa believed he might find an organ to repair on Bora Bora if she lived there. "What if I told you, since all I need to do this semester is a few papers and present my MFA review papers, that I don't have to be at the school full-time?"

"Where would you go?"

"Well, I heard the blizzard sent a tree through a church window in New Rochelle, so I emailed them my bid yesterday."

"As in New Rochelle, the town on Long Island? You're going to come back?"

"I kind of hoped their organ needed work too, so I could recommend this guy I met. He would come, and maybe we could go on a date. And after that another one?"

"I don't know. There are several organ tuners in the city, some of them in committed relationships already."

Tessa stepped back but kept her hands on his chest. "I don't think this one is."

"Obviously, there must be something wrong with my explanations." Sean lowered his head.

Tessa met him halfway. Not a single thing was wrong with his explanations—until Candace interrupted with a very loud, very fake cough.

Sean and Tessa turned toward the intruders and were surprised to realize they had drawn a small crowd.

The girl in the wig spoke first. "Hi, I am Candace, and you are kissing my roommate, so I think you'd better introduce yourself."

Sean shook hands as names flew by too fast to catch.

A man that looked like he could be security held onto his hand longer than necessary. Sean was sure the man was trying to say something with his firm grip. "I don't recall a Cavanagh on the invitation list. Do you, Allie?"

A woman who stood next to the security guard shook her head. "May I see your invitation?"

Sean pulled the invitation from his pocket.

"How did you get Nick Gooding's invitation?"

Tessa's grip on his arm tightened. Before Sean could answer, Daniel Crawford and his wife entered the circle. "So, you're the guy Nick texted me about. It's fine, Mr. Alexander and Allie, he isn't a party crasher. A friend of mine gave Sean his invitation in case he arrived too late to be Tessa's plus-one."

As the security team faded into the background, Daniel turned to Sean and extended his hand. "Welcome to Chicago. And a word of warning—break Tessa's heart, and my wife will cry too. I am not fond of her tears, so I will probably send Alex and his sister after you. And don't be fooled. Allie is probably the deadlier of the two." If Daniel hadn't ended the sentence with a huge smile, Sean might have felt compelled to defend himself.

Mandy finally shook his hand. "Did you drive out or fly?"

"I drove."

"Were you able to get a hotel room? I believe there are a couple unclaimed in the block we rented."

"A woman named Bonnie called me this morning and gave me a room."

Mandy turned to an older woman. "I thought you retired."

Bonnie shrugged. "It is hard to do, so I get Daniel to give me a little something, like coordinating rooms for family and friends at the annual party."

"Well, I think it's time we leave these two alone. I am quite sure we interrupted a discussion, and there is less than a half hour till the New Year!" Candace led the group off but not before Sean caught her wink at Tessa.

A love ballad was playing. "Shall we dance?" Sean didn't wait for an answer. He wasn't going to let Tessa get away before midnight. He had some pretty specific New Year's resolutions, and making his relationship with Tessa permanent sat at the top of the list. How many more times would he need to explain things to her?

Tessa slipped into his arms, and they glided around the ballroom. "Where did you learn to dance?"

"Mom. She loved to dance ballroom, so after Dad passed, I became her partner."

"I hope she doesn't mind if I don't share you too often."

Sean led them into a spin. "I think she can live with it. Richard does dance."

"Good, because I think I am learning to enjoy it."

"Then I shall ask you out dancing the next time you come to New York."

"Our first date?"

"No." Sean spun her out and back.

Tessa tilted her head. "What do you mean, no?"

"I mean I intend to take you out to breakfast in the morning for our first date. We have a lot to talk about."

"So are you going to ask me?"

"I thought I just did."

Tessa shook her head, making her curls bob. "A question needs a question mark at the end."

"Oh. Will you have break—?"

"Ten. Nine. Eight. Seven. Six. Five. Four. Three. Two. One !"

Cheers erupted around them as Sean finished asking the question with a kiss.

epilogue

Good Friday at the Church of the Nativity

Tessa threw her arms around Sean. "You played it perfectly! How long has it been since the entire *Messiah* has been performed here?"

"I'm not sure. So many people don't think about the other two parts. But we haven't done an Easter Concert since I was a boy."

"I especially enjoyed "The Trumpet Shall Sound." It reminded me of all those Christmas miracles. Too bad Granda couldn't be here."

"From the sound of his last text, he is having too much fun exploring Ireland."

"Maybe he can kiss the Blarney Stone and get an accent."

Sean let Tessa go and gathered up his music. "I hope this kicks off a great summer concert series."

"How could it not? You are in charge. I know these last few months have been hard for you, but being chairman of the museum board seems to suit you. And you are doing a pretty good job of figuring the rest out."

When he had told her the news of his changed tax bracket last New Year's Day, she hadn't believed him. Things like that just didn't happen. But after her visiting him the next weekend in Blue Pines, flying first class, she accepted the inconceivable reality. When he offered to build her a glass workshop, Tessa chose to go into partnership with Daniel with the caveat that Sean could buy him out if her relationship became permanent. For that reason, she chose an old Blue Pines warehouse as the location. Tessa followed him to the office, which was now much cleaner than in Granda's day.

"I still wake up and pinch myself. Just the thought that I could walk out of the door and purchase almost anything I want blows my mind. But then I read an email like the one from that odious little rector in the Bronx asking for money to replace their ill-treated organ and it becomes all too real. I'm glad you have been by my side to keep me grounded."

Tessa laughed. "I don't think telling you to wait to purchase a Lamborghini until you had a garage is keeping you grounded. But it has been nice to get the best seats at all the Broadway shows and fly out here to see you as often as I wanted to."

Sean pulled her into a hug. "I can't wait for graduation when you are out here for good. A week for spring break is not enough." He kissed her. She returned the kiss. Money or not, in his arms was her favorite place to be.

She ended the kiss. "I'm just happy that Professor Christensen is doing better, not that I minded subbing. But, I am definitely done with school. I can't wait for graduation."

Sean held out his hand. "There is something I want to show you."

Tessa followed him down into the catacombs. In the center of the table in room four sat an unmarked banker's box. "Did I miss one when I cleaned down here?"

"Open it."

The lid wasn't dusty. Tessa set it to one side. Billows of white lace fluffed out of the box. And Tessa lifted out an intricate veil.

"My great-grandmother wore it, and then my grandmother, and my mother. Since Mom didn't have any girls, she gave it to me."

Tessa carefully lifted the cloth from the box. "Oh, my. This is—it's beyond beautiful."

"Will you wear it for me?"

"Now?" Tessa thought she knew what he was asking but wanted to make sure.

Sean shook his head. "No. More like in a couple of months, upstairs, in the chapel."

She tucked the veil back into the box. "Is this a proposal?"

"You can't tell?"

Tessa smiled big and shook her head. "I've only heard you ask me to wear the veil in the chapel. I am a bit unclear."

Sean grabbed Tessa by the waist and set her on the table where they were eye to eye. "Tessa Doyle, I'm asking you—no, I am begging you to be my bride."

Tessa didn't answer. Instead she wrapped her arms around him and kissed him until he understood.

The End

acknowledgments

For five amazing weeks in 2016 I was privileged to work on the Roots of Knowledge window as a temporary member of the Holdman Studios team. A huge thank you to Tom Holdman for teaching me about stained glass and answering questions for me. I suggest that all my readers take an hour or two at the UVU Library or look at the window on-line: www.uvu.edu/rootsofknowledge.

Good roommates make lifelong friends. I am lucky enough to have Ronnie Bishop as one of those. She spent hours texting and educating me about organs. She along with her husband Rich provided amazing insight in to the world of organs and then tried to correct all of my mistakes.

This book would not exist without the encouragement of Cindy to whom this book is dedicated. Translation: *There is nothing on this earth more to be prized than true friendship.*

Huge thanks to my beta readers and proof readers especially Nanette for her willingness to read things so many times. I would never make it through a day without Sally whose advice keeps me going. Thanks to all the writers in Cache Valley League of Utah writers, and iWriteNetwork, each of you has made me a better writer. Thank you for your part in my growth as a fledging writer.

Thanks also to Michele at Eschler Editing for the edits and finding oh so many little things to fix; any mistakes left in this book are not her fault. Nor are my excellent proofreaders to be blamed. Thank you ladies and gents!

My family, for sharing their home with the fictional characters who often got fed better than they did. And my husband who encouraged me every crazy step of the way, and who is my example for every love story I dream up. The real one is better.

And to my Father in Heaven for putting these wonderful people, and any I may have forgotten to mention, in my life. I am grateful for every experience and blessing I have been granted.

about the author

LORIN GRACE WAS BORN IN Colorado and has been moving around the country ever since, living in eight states and several imaginary worlds. She graduated from Brigham Young University with a degree in Graphic Design.

Currently she lives in northern Utah with her husband, four children, and a dog who is insanely jealous of her laptop. When not writing Lorin enjoys creating graphics, visiting historical sites, museums, and reading.

Lorin is an active member of the League of Utah Writers and was awarded Honorable Mention in their 2016 creative writing contest short romance story category. Her debut novel, *Waking Lucy*, was awarded a 2017 Recommend Read award in the LUW Published book contest.

You can learn more about her, and sign up for her writers club at loringrace.com or at Facebook: LorinGraceWriter

www.ingramcontent.com/pod-product-compliance
Lightning Source LLC
Chambersburg PA
CBHW060122260626
47160CB00005B/1983